RUBBING ONE OUT

SUSAN MAC NICOL

ALSO BY SUSAN MAC NICOL

THE STARLIGHT SERIES
Cassandra by Starlight
Together in Starlight
Forever in Starlight

THE MEN OF LONDON SERIES
Love You Senseless
Sight & Sinners
Suit Yourself
Feat of Clay
Cross to Bare
Flying Solo
Damaged Goods
Hard Climate
Survival Game
Not So Secret Santa

FETISH ALLEY SERIES
For Fox Sake
Death By C*ck
Cover Me in Chocolate

OTHER TITLES
Stripped Bare
Saving Alexander
Worth Keeping
Double Alchemy
Double Alchemy: Climax
Love and Punishment
Sight Unseen

Unlikely in Love
Living On Air
Soul of Discretion
Promises Kept
Gin Me Over

www.BOROUGHSPUBLISHINGGROUP.com

PUBLISHER'S NOTE: This is a work of fiction. Names, characters, places and incidents either are the product of the author's imagination or are used fictitiously. Any resemblance to actual events, locales, business establishments or persons, living or dead, is coincidental. Boroughs Publishing Group does not have any control over and does not assume responsibility for author or third-party websites, blogs or critiques or their content.

RUBBING ONE OUT

Copyright © 2021 Susan Elaine Mac Nicol

ISBN 978-1-953810-41-0

To everyone who's ever wished upon a star or rubbed that lamp in the charity shop or flea market – this hope is for the extraordinary lives in us all, and despite the daily grind of reality, we want to believe magic <u>does</u> exist

ACKNOWLEDGMENTS

To the wonderful staff at Colchester Zoo here in Essex who gave me the opportunity to meet their penguins personally. I was "Keeper for the Day" at the zoo, with the focus on these amazing birds. The *real* keeper was patient, knowledgeable, and answered all my questions. I even got to feed the greedy little blighters.

Also, I'd like to thank my readers for waiting patiently for me to write another book. I'm hoping to give you a lot more in 2021 so stay in touch and I'll do my best to surprise you.

RUBBING ONE OUT

Chapter 1

Ten minutes I've been doing this. Ten fucking minutes.

Ben shivered as he stood on the edge of the rock pool in the penguin enclosure at Windward Zoo in Winchester. In a cartoon world, steam would be puffing through his ears together with the all-too-real vapour trail from his breath. It was early March and still chilly.

He'd been trying to coax one of the animals over to him to give her medication—an anti-malarial pill contained in a silvery sprat. The recalcitrant bird eyed him balefully as yet another floating herring found its way into her greedy gullet.

Ben took a deep, calming breath, trying to contain his urge to commit birdie murder. Or was it called birdiecide?

"Honey, for the last time, get the fuck into the water and come over here before I make a penguin pie out of you. How do you fancy being covered in nice, warm pastry?"

Threatening her didn't help. Honey wasn't having any of it. The Humboldt penguin blinked at him innocently and stayed in the middle of the large rock perch immersed in the pool. If a penguin could bat eyelashes at a man in a *fuck you* gesture, Ben was watching the bird do it.

He was sure the other penguins gathered beside him on the beach were enjoying his predicament. He thought he'd heard a couple of them snicker. Comments were also forthcoming from the peanut gallery where the visitors stood. One young kid, he couldn't have been more than fourteen, had shouted, "I hope you don't have the same trouble with your women, mate."

He wanted to growl at the little sod and correct him. Men, not women, thank you very much. He didn't have trouble in that area, but he manfully held off.

"Honey, come on over. Now." His growl didn't have the desired effect. He huffed then changed his strategy.

"If you come on out, I'll give you an extra anchovy for supper," he coaxed. The penguin didn't think much of that reward. She looked at him, seeming to consider the options. Then Honey dipped her head and dove into the depths of the water—on the far side of the enclosure.

"Fuck," Ben said, then looked around guiltily. Up on the observation deck, several eager toddlers and parents were watching, but he didn't think anyone had heard him.

"Fine," he called across the expanse of shimmering water. "I'm leaving now, and I'll make sure at feeding time later you get the smallest fishes. The bigger ones can go to Dolly because, unlike you, she does as she's told."

The crowd above laughed, no doubt enjoying the battle of wills. Ben huffed and turned away, hearing the splashes of wings in the water behind him. He didn't turn around. Instead, he pretended to open the gate to leave, and fiddled with the latch in the hope Honey would see sense.

Out of the corner of his eye, he saw the penguin jump out of the water and waddle off towards her fellow penguins. He smiled in triumph as she eyed him with suspicion. Eddie, one of the smaller of the penguins, squawked beside him, his wings flapping wildly.

"I know, buddy," Ben said soothingly. "She's a real pain in the arse, isn't she? Imagine if she was *your* mother."

Honey was mom to a cuter, smaller version of herself, a young male the zoo had named Taffy. He was adorable, and way more good-natured than his parent.

Whatever Eddie had said to Honey worked. She trundled over to Ben, and he took the opportunity to feed her the sprat. The troublemaker swallowed it down and looked at him expectantly.

"That wasn't so bad, was it?" Ben grumbled. "There's no more for you. You're still getting the smallest fishes later." He stuck out his tongue at the birds staring at him and then looked around to check no one had seen the infantile gesture. Being seen to threaten penguins with promises of lesser fish and resorting to childish tactics at the ripe age of thirty-two wouldn't do his professional credentials much good.

He had an MSci in zoology, and several years' experience in field studies around the world, yet being senior keeper for the penguins, and often the seals, was a job he loved. He had a special affinity for the cheeky birds.

Even if they do make me curse at them now and then.

***

When his workday was over, Ben decided to pop into one of his favourite places: Craxton Mill in Winchester. The old site held many memories for him. When he was a child, his antique-hunting, eccentric parents had taken him along on their trails to find the next Van Gogh in a boot sale, or a forgotten first edition in a cluttered second-hand shop. Ben had inherited the bug. Nothing soothed him more than rummaging around in places that might offer treasures from another person's castoffs.

There was also the sense of history and magic in finding old relics. They spoke stories from their years on earth.

Ben was a lover of all things supernatural and magical. No doubt he'd inherited it from his mother, who had regaled his bedtime reading with tales of fairies, pixies, and Ben's personal favourite, elves. One only had to look now at the gorgeous Orlando Bloom in *Lord of the Rings* to understand *that* obsession.

As he cycled the eight or so miles down country lanes alongside the beautiful South Downs National Park, and into the historic town of Wickham, set in the scenic Meon Valley, Ben marvelled at how fortunate he was to live here.

He'd been born and bred in the area, as had his parents and their parents, and the Sinclair family tree reached back hundreds of years. His dad lived in a small bungalow, not too far away. His mom had passed away ten years ago, and they both still missed her.

He parked and chained up his bike outside the cracked redbrick façade of the old mill. He might live in a sleepy village, but thieves still abounded. Usually, the young teenage kind who fancied a joyride. He left his riding gloves and jacket on because the shop was cold as fuck. The owner, old man Jenkins, was a bit of a stingy tosser who didn't see the benefit of heaters.

As Ben entered the shop, the proprietor's son, Ryan, looked up from the purchases he was ringing up, and beamed at him.

"Ben. Give me a minute and I'll be right with you." Ryan looked down at the goods on the counter, and Ben swore he worked faster to get the poor customer out of the way.

Ben sighed. Ryan was twenty-one, eager, and thought Ben was the answer to his gay prayers. Ben wasn't fond of people using his full name, but Ryan had fallen into the habit of using it because he said it sounded sexier. Ryan was tasty in a Billy Gilman kind of way, but he wasn't to Ben's liking. Ben had a fetish for dark, sexy eyebrows and lean, sinewy bodies. Ryan played fullback in the local rugby team and was rather beefy.

Ben ambled over to a particularly quirky display of antique candelabra and lamps. His cottage could do with a new light for his bedside table. His old one had fallen over and cracked after a rather riotous bout of hook-up sex with an old friend with benefits. Darrall had been rather creative in his endeavours to prove he could suck his own cock. The pair of them had been in hysterics when it had all gone masterfully wrong. Flailing limbs and acrobatic contortions were not conducive to the layout in Ben's cosy bedroom.

He picked up a couple of items, perusing them with interest then setting them down. He didn't think he was in the market for a blown-glass lampshade, no matter how pretty it was when the colours sparkled in the sunlight. Behind him, Ryan was trying to sell an antique walking stick to an older man. Ben grinned.

Ryan's sales patter could do with a little finesse. Ben didn't think saying "This will help you with those old bones of yours" would endear him to the customer, especially seeing who the customer was. Albert Finkelstein was a crabby old blighter at the best of times. Ben sniggered when Albert replied testily, "Now look here, you whippersnapper, that's enough of that ageist talk. You should be ashamed of yourself."

Still chuckling, Ben reached back to the rear of the shelf, knocking something over by accident. The item fell to the floor with a clang, and Ben froze. The shop had a firm *Damage Me, Buy Me* policy and he didn't think he wanted…a brass lamp.

He bent down, casting a furtive glance at Ryan, who still looked as if he was feeling the wrath of Albert's sharp tongue. Ben picked up the lamp in his gloved hands and scrutinised it carefully. It looked undamaged, thank fuck. The price tag said twenty pounds and Ben certainly didn't think he was in the market for something quirky, which had no real purpose.

It was a charming brass piece, Ben acknowledged. It bore no visible hallmark and was delightfully designed with a small chain anchoring the lid to the handle. He weighed the heavy little piece in his hand, growing fonder of it as the seconds passed. There was something about it captured his imagination, reminding him of the Aladdin and the Genie tale from *1001 Arabian Nights*.

As a boy, Ben had loved hearing those tales when his mom had read to him at night. At one time in his childhood fantasies, he'd gone through a stage of pretending to have a flying carpet. Luckily, his more practical father had managed to get to him before he leapt off the garage roof to prove he could fly. At the time he'd been upset at being thwarted, but as an adult, he realised that the two-storey fall would've probably killed him.

Casting a glance around the store to see no one was watching, he rubbed the lamp furtively. *You never know, right?* He was disappointed when nothing happened.

Another childhood story shot down in flames, he reflected in disappointment. Maybe there was an art to it, even some magic words to be said.

"Open Sesame," he whispered as he rubbed the lamp again. Nothing. Maybe it didn't work because he was wearing gloves.

Ben huffed. Even though it didn't work, the lamp had grown on him. He had to have it. The feeling of possession was overwhelming.

Perhaps he could use his masculine wiles to talk Ryan down from the tag price. After all, what was the point of being a sex bomb to a younger man if you didn't use it to your advantage?

He walked over to Ryan, who'd extricated himself from his tricky situation but looked a little worse for wear.

"Geesh," Ryan muttered as he gave Ben a slow, approving appraisal from top to toe, all six foot two of him. "Mr Finkelstein is a crabby arsehole sometimes. All I wanted to do was tell him about this fancy walking stick."

Ben laughed. "Yeah, I heard him. He has a way with words, that's for sure." He leaned over the counter, hoping his Paco Rabanne aftershave tantalised Ryan's nostrils. He'd also undone one of the buttons on his shirt to let a peek of his dark blond chest hair peek through. He knew he filled out his black jeans well enough, and his blue eyes seemed to be a draw for most men.

I'm such a man-slut, he thought wryly. Ryan's gaze was drawn to Ben's chest as he licked his lips.

"I found this over there," Ben gestured to the lamp, then the shelf, "I wondered if I could get it for less than the price tag? It's a cute piece and reminds me of when I was a kid. Childhood memories are such a special thing." He grinned and noticed with satisfaction something he was doing certainly buzzed Ryan's drill. Ben ran his hand through his short, styled hair slowly, like he was the guy in the Paco Rabanne commercial. *As if.*

"Oh, I'm not sure," Ryan hedged, his gaze drawn to Ben's hand then back to his chest. "My dad would probably kill me if I let it go for less. He brought that back from a trip to the Middle East."

"Huh." Ryan's dad Glenn was rather a stickler for the rules. Ben stretched his arms up, making sure it made the most of his torso, and his shirt lifted a *teeny* bit to show pale skin beneath. Ryan's eyes bugged out. "I thought perhaps you could make an exception for me. Seeing as how we're friends."

Ryan's Adam's apple bobbed up and down as he swallowed. "I guess, perhaps I could take a fiver off the price. But no more, or honestly, Dad will skin me."

Ben considered the offer, then grinned. He didn't want to be responsible for anything bad befalling Ryan. He might not want to date the guy, but he *was* cute. "Done." He reached out to shake Ryan's sweaty palm. "Thanks for that."

Ben took out his wallet, removed a dirty ten and a five-pound note and laid them on the counter. "I have just the place on the mantelpiece for this. It needs a bit of a polish, but I'm sure with a touch of Brasso, it'll come up sparkling. Although I have to say, I quite like the old look. I might dust it off and leave it at that."

Ryan rang the sale up and passed the receipt and the lamp in a paper bag over to Ben. "You must have quite a collection of stuff now. You're always in here." His voice held a tinge of longing. "Um, is it only the items in the shop you come in for, or is there something else drawing your attention?" The underlying something or someone didn't escape Ben. He felt like a heel, but he needed to head this off at the pass before Ryan got the wrong idea.

"I'm always on the prowl for unusual stuff. It's why I love this shop so much. My parents were big collectors, so I grew up with it. And…" he hesitated, "forgive me, but I'm not interested in any sort of relationship right now if that's what you're asking?"

"Oh, no problem," Ryan stuttered, turning crimson. "I didn't mean to imply anything. I mean I didn't think you'd be interested…" He trailed off, looking rather woebegone. Ben had to give the kid *some* sort of ego boost.

He leaned over the counter and patted Ryan's shoulder. "You'll find the right guy one day because you're a real catch. You're cute, friendly, and you're young. Men will be queueing up to take you out one of these days."

Ryan eyed him moodily. "This is Wickham," he said gloomily. "I don't even know any other gay guys around here."

Ben winked wickedly. "Then let me educate you a little." He pulled out his wallet and retrieved a tatty card. "Here, this is a place I know in Winchester, not too far from here. It's a cool spot, not a dive, so you'll be okay there. Tell the bouncer—his name is Steve— you know me, and he'll look after you."

Ryan took the cards. "Honestly? I don't go out much, so I have no idea what to do." His face turned hopeful. "Say, would you come with me the first time? As friends?"

Ben cleared his throat. He supposed he could show the baby gay the ropes a little. "Sure. Maybe next weekend? Gives you time to see what's in your wardrobe. You know, tight jeans, tight shirt, and all that jazz. You can't go wrong." He turned to leave, bag clutched in his hand. "See you next weekend then, Ryan. I'll give you a call. I have the shop number."

"Cheers," Ryan called out as Ben headed out. "I'm looking forward to it."

As Ben cycled home with his treasure, he hoped Ryan hadn't read more into his offer.

Chapter 2

Home at last in his cosy two-bedroom thatched cottage, Ben sighed in relief as he got out of his jacket and gloves, leaving them in an untidy pile on the dining room table. He strolled into the kitchen over to the fridge and retrieved a beer. He popped the tab, took a slug, and sighed in satisfaction. *That hits the spot.*

He'd hardly had time to drink the first sip when a bundle of black fur tackled him waist-high, and a wet tongue licked him from jaw to temple.

"Tess, how are you doing, baby?" Ben ruffled the dog's fur as she climbed down. "Did you have a good day?"

Tess sat smiling up at him, her brown eyes filled with love. She was a rescue Labrador, and Ben's best part about coming home. A human had never greeted him with as much enthusiasm as she did each day.

He checked Tess had fresh water and kibble, then made his way into the adjoining lounge, Tess trotting behind him. It was quaint. A proper bachelor pad with only what was needed: an armchair, a two-seater couch, a couple of small side tables, and a set of bookshelves along the wall that didn't slope down. His fifty-nine-inch television took pride of place in the corner.

Upstairs were two small bedrooms and a bathroom. It was everything Ben needed.

He slumped into his favourite chair. One he'd rescued from a flea market. It was a huge, floppy fabric affair of biscuit-coloured comfort and Ben loved nothing more than to stretch out on it after a hard day's work and watch a David Attenborough programme.

He took another drink and put his feet up on the rustic centre coffee table (yet another buy from a flea market). Tess settled comfortably at his feet although she did give him a disdainful stare.

"I'll take you for a walk in a minute. Let me finish my beer."

It was comforting to come home to someone, even if it was a fur baby, although his lounge was starting to look more like an animal haven than an adult's dwelling. Tess's toys littered the floor—old socks, half-chewed rope toys, and a manky old duck toy she loved. Home to Ben's aging guinea pig, Pookums, was a cage in the corner—a medium-size wooden structure behind wire, resembling a tiny comfortable log cabin, with walkways and exercise areas. It cramped the room a little, but Ben would have it no other way.

Currently, Pookums, who was seven years old, lay on the bottom of the cage, curled up and snoring. Ben knew his little friend didn't have long left. He'd inherited the silly-named animal from his niece, Lucy, when his brother had taken his family abroad to Australia. She'd been devastated leaving her little friend behind, but Ben had promised to take care of him.

He reached down idly and scratched his belly. He supposed he should be thinking about making himself something to eat, but he honestly couldn't be bothered. Being an admitted lazy chef, he was content to eat microwave meals and live on pastries and fast food. He was lucky he had a fast metabolism, or he'd be the size of the Michelin Man by now. Grunting, he got up to putter about in the kitchen to see what was there. As he brushed past his backpack, there was a loud clang. He turned to see the lamp he'd bought swivelling slowly on the floor as if it were playing a game of spin the bottle.

He bent down to pick it up and was again struck by the ornate patterns on the brass. There were swirls of what looked like angel wings against a cloudy sky. The little teapot-like lid had come loose, tethered to the handle by a delicate brass chain. Ben wondered what the lamp had once carried. Precious oils perhaps for a gentleman or lady faring overseas by a wind-sailed boat, or possibly scented tea for the Grand Poo-Bah of an elite desert sect with a harem of cute men to service his every need.

Huh. Where the heck did that come from? It's only a lamp, you silly tosser.

He sniffed the opening and could detect a whiff of something spicy, sandalwood perhaps, and another odour he couldn't quite identify, which made him close his eyes and imagine dirty thoughts. It invoked the scent of a man's skin, the soft tendrils of his hair, and the enticing thrill of warm flesh against his. Ben could feel long, experienced fingers grasping him and slicking him to completion…

"Jesus," he gasped, and he drew away in aroused panic. "What the hell?"

Inside his jeans, his cock made its enjoyment of the tantalising experience known, and Ben pressed a hand against his groin. "Calm down, you. It's an old oil lamp, not a naked Tom Hiddleston. There's no need for that kind of reaction."

He sniffed cautiously at the lamp again, but the fragrance seemed to have disappeared. "Huh," he said thoughtfully. "Perhaps you *do* have a bit of magic in you after all." He put the lamp on the table and fetched another beer, completely forgetting he'd originally been heading to find something to eat.

Ben glowered at the lamp as he drank his beer and wondered what had happened to give him a chub. He didn't *mind* so much as not knowing what had prompted his out-of-control reaction. He tended to be something of a control freak.

The low-pitched wood-framed windows in the lounge looked out onto a large stretch of garden, complete with stream, and a field, beyond which was his closest neighbour. Christine was a hardworking farmer, a woman in her sixties who laboured like a Trojan and could be seen out every morning before the cock crowed. Because the cock *did* crow, unfortunately. Like clockwork at six-thirty in the morning. Her rooster, Tricky Dicky (Ben still had to find out how the damned bird had got his name), perched on the wooden fence separating the two properties. With great gusto, he'd then proceed to give a raucous rendition of cock crows, which seemed to go on forever. At last count, five before the poxy rooster had stopped his morning celebrations. *The joys of country living.*

Ben loved his home. Colourful hollyhocks grew in abandon, fruit trees scattered their pink and white blossoms across the border of his property, and the fishpond under the trees was home to ducks and frogs alike. It was tranquil, private, and he wouldn't want to live anywhere else.

"C'mon, Tess, let's have a stroll before I'm too tired to stand." An admitted workaholic, he put in long hours, which took their toll.

That night, when he settled into his comfy king-size bed with Tess next to him, he drew the feather duvet over his head, feeling a sense of anticipation about tomorrow. Why? He had no idea.

As he fell asleep, he hugged his pillow close and smiled. Tomorrow was going to be a good day.

***

"This has got to be the shittiest day on record," Ben groaned, as he wrestled a large new water pump into place in the currently empty seal enclosure. "Jesus, this thing weighs a fucking ton."

"Keep pushing," puffed Hemingway Dube, Ben's colleague and best friend. His full lips were pushed back from his teeth in a white snarl as he strained to hold the pump in place while Ben anchored it. "I don't want my beautiful black self to become mashed against the concrete, my friend. My girlfriends would cry too much, and there would be much gnashing of teeth."

He gave a wide grin as Ben managed to get out a snort in between his heavy breathing. "You overestimate yourself, Hem. I've seen your girlfriends, and I think they'll hold a party. Finally, they'll be able to get together and rag on what a two-timer you were."

Hem had a penchant for dating more than one woman at a time. He'd told Ben it was an ancestral benefit dating back many years for a man to have many women. While Ben didn't doubt that tradition existed, he didn't think having affairs with multiple women at once was what had been intended.

"You are jealous because you cannot find even one boyfriend. You are too picky," Hem proclaimed as he secured the steel straps around the pump. His impressive biceps strained with the effort. Hemmy wasn't a small man. "Okay, you can let go now. I think we have done it."

Ben stepped back, still wary of the mammoth structure falling. When it stayed put, Hemingway chuckled loudly and stroked his stubbled beard. "See? I told you it would only take two of us. I am the stronger one among us, but I was glad of your help."

Ben rolled his aching shoulders, ignoring the bait his friend left hanging. "Shit, that was heavy. I think I might have a hernia." He scowled. "What a day for the damn pump to give up the ghost. I know the boss intended installing the new one he'd bought, but I didn't think we'd have to do it quite this soon."

Hemingway gave a philosophical shrug. "It is what I am here for. I have you as my apprentice, so we make a good team."

Hemingway also had a degree in zoology from the University of Pretoria in SA and was one of the life support technicians for the zoo. He loved anything to do with engineering and tinkering with parts. Mechanical bits floated his boat. Last time he'd visited Ben, he'd messed about with the toaster, which had stubbornly refused to heat up. Now the thing worked like a charm.

Ben enjoyed getting his hands dirty, and being out in the sunshine with a man he called a good friend was always welcome.

"Talking of boyfriends…" Hemingway said slyly as he plopped himself down on the grass and reached into his overall pocket for a forbidden cigarette. "When was the last time you got laid?"

Ben glared at him. "None of your fucking business. Just because you like notches on your belt doesn't mean I do."

Hemingway nodded wisely, puffing on his cigarette. "Ah, so that would mean a long time ago. Do not be embarrassed, my friend." He waved down at his lean physique. "Not everyone can be a sexy powerhouse like me."

Ben sat down on the grass next to him, trying to shield Hemingway from the public footpath. If his boss, Hazel, caught him smoking again in public, there'd be hell to pay. His friend didn't seem to acknowledge the danger, or if he did, he didn't care.

"More like a fizzled-out sparkler, you are," Ben teased, eying out the long legs of a tasty park visitor as he strode past. The man had an arse to be proud of. "You know I'm no player, Hem. Until I find the right guy, I'm fine with my own company."

That wasn't *strictly* true. Ben had the occasional hook-up when he was feeling the need, but it wasn't anything serious, or something he relished.

"You are such a romantic." Hemingway took one final puff of his smoke then buried the butt end in the dark soil of the nearest garden bed. "You're thirty-two years old and still waiting for your prince to come." His tone was teasing. "I applaud your sentiments, but sometimes a man simply needs to let off some steam. You should find yourself a friend with benefits." He grinned. "How about that young man down at the antiques store? Didn't you say he had his eye on you?"

Ben snorted. "Ryan? He's a nice guy, but there's no chemistry. Besides, he's only twenty-one."

Hemingway clapped a dramatic hand to his forehead. "Oh, the shame," he sang out. "An eleven-year difference. What would the neighbours think?" He snorted loudly. "I'll tell you what they'd think seeing that tasty young man going into your home. They'd say Ben Sinclair had finally got over himself and scheduled a good fuck. God knows you need one."

Ben narrowed his eyes then launched himself at his friend, who laughed in merriment as they rolled around on the grass. Hemingway had a ticklish spot between his ribs, and Ben was hell-bound on getting the man to squeal like a ferret.

Finally, panting in exertion, Ben lay back on the grass, Hemingway lying next to him, also short of breath.

"Well," Hemingway panted, "I wasn't intending being your play-pal of the day, but I guess wrestling with me is the closest *you're* getting to sex today." He jumped up nimbly, out of reach of Ben's fingers reaching over to do more damage.

Hemingway brushed the grass of his overalls and reached out a hand to help Ben to his feet. "Come on. It's almost home time. I'll buy you a pint at the pub. If you're lucky, maybe even a packet of crisps. We'll call it a reverse date. The physical stuff first then the dinner." He guffawed loudly.

Ben smiled at him as he clambered up. "You're a douche, you know that? But I'll take you up on the dinner date. I could use a beer." It'd mean he'd have to get a taxi home, instead of using his bicycle, but what the hell. Perhaps Hemmy could pick him up in the morning.

Getting tipsy sounded like a damned good idea.

Chapter 3

The tinkling of bells nudged Ben awake from a deep sleep. He snuffled into his pillow, stretched his legs beneath the duvet, which was a little awkward as Tess was lumbered on top, and closed his eyes.

"Bloody wind chimes," he mumbled. "Need to move them tomorrow." He'd no sooner found a comfy spot when the bells rang again. It didn't sound like the usual tinkling. Ben rousted himself once again and listened. It seemed as if the chimes were sounding from *inside* the house. To his knowledge, he had no bell instruments or gadgets. Perhaps it was his mobile. He'd probably left it next to his armchair in the lounge, and something was chiming. Maybe it was a Facebook or Instagram message.

The clock on his bedside table read three a.m. He thumped his pillow and settled down again. Tess hadn't even stirred, and continued to snore softly.

No sooner had he gotten comfortable, the bells went again. Not once, not twice, but three times.

"Shit," he swore as he got out of bed, starkers. "I leave my phone away from the bedroom for a reason. What twat is shoving his shit on Facebook at this time of the morning?"

It was Saturday, and he'd been looking forward to a lie-in, followed by making himself a carb-laden English breakfast.

Growling under his breath, he stormed through to the lounge and saw his phone lying innocently on the side of the couch. Ben picked it up, switched it off, and threw it back down.

As he started back to bed, the bells rang again. Ben stopped. He wasn't afraid to admit a cold sliver of something unwelcome slid down his spine. He'd seen those films where you disconnected the telly, yet it still went on showing static, and then creepy voices spoke before everything literally went to hell.

He cleared his throat quietly and stood, waiting to see where the sound was coming from. After a few seconds, it went again. It seemed to be coming from the cabinet in the dining room. Ben took a deep breath and sidled over to it. All he had on the shelves were some books, a box of old chocolates with all the caramels remaining—he wasn't a fan of those—some tattered textbooks from university, a roll of chewing gum, a plaque someone had given him of a cute koala saying, "I have the koalifications," and the brass lamp he'd found at the antiques store. Nothing bell- or tinkly-like at all.

He bent down closer to listen, and as he did, something warm and fragrant blew into his ear. He jerked back, heart beating like thunder. "What the fuck?" The air smelt faintly of incense, conjuring up vague thoughts of Arabian nights and a warm desert.

Ben wasn't a fanciful man, and that he saw camels and palm trees in his head was unsettling, even creepy.

A thin tendril of what looked like smoke emanated from the spout of the brass lamp. Ben swallowed and reached out to pick it up. Perhaps there'd been a remnant of something smoky trapped inside when he'd bought it, and it was only now expelling, he reasoned. He couldn't think of any other cause for the object to be smoking.

The brass lamp was warm to the touch and seemed to glow faintly. Ben reached out one trembling finger and touched the side of it. Where could the heat be coming from? Feeling a little braver, he rubbed the side of the lamp gently, then increased the pressure.

The air around him deadened and his ears popped with a strange sensation. It felt like he was on an aeroplane, taking off. Ben clicked his jaw twice to relieve the pressure. As he did, the brass lamp grew scalding hot, and he dropped it to the floor.

"Motherfucker," he exclaimed as the tingle in his fingers intensified. "The bloody thing is trying to set me on fire." He sucked his index finger then shrieked in terror when a voice behind him said in amusement, "I thought *I* was the one granting the wishes. Instead, I get my very own wet dream."

Ben was too busy hyperventilating to register the sultry tone of whatever—whoever was behind him. He was afraid to turn around in case something with a pronged tail and horns stood there.

"Who the fuck are you?" he managed at last, his bare arse still in full view of the stranger. "What are you doing in my house?"

There was a soft chuckle. "Turn around so I can see if the front matches the back. If it does, I'll be one happy Djinn."

"Your name's Jim?" Ben asked in confusion. "You don't sound like a Jim." The voice sounded male, but had a faint accent, softly Middle Eastern.

Whoever/whatever it was sighed in exasperation. "Djinn, you fool. As in genie? We prefer the word Djinn. Modern folk take all the fun out of the old words."

I must be dreaming. Any minute now I'll wake up.

Ben turned slowly, his hand picking up a heavy textbook in case he needed a weapon. When he saw who stood before him, his jaw dropped.

A young man, probably in his late twenties, stood staring at him in amusement. He was bare-chested and smooth—Ben couldn't help but notice a pair of pierced nipples—and a tight pair of black silky trousers, which left little to the imagination. His arms were tattooed, and a strange chain bracelet stretched from a band around his sexy bicep to a leather band around his wrist. His hair was dark burgundy, blended with lighter streaks, and was cut in stylish swathes, which swung around his fine-boned cheeks.

Oh my God, Ben thought when his eyes lit on the man's crotch. He has *a lot* to be proud of. *That body. Those eyes. What colour are they? Purple? No. More incredible than that. And he's wearing kohl. Fuck, it looks hot. Wait. What the hell is he doing here should be the question. Focus.*

The sublime being before him raised one perfect eyebrow. "Hmm, I like what I see. You certainly have promise. I can tell you're not immune to my charms." The man—if that's what he was—winked at Ben and gestured to Ben's groin. Ben looked down and felt his face erupt in flames.

"Fuck, I'm naked. I forgot. This isn't for you, whatever you are. This is what we call a morning glory, you know, when you're rudely woken up by strangers coming into your house and don't have a chance to, like, get rid of it."

The *person*—Ben still wasn't sure whether he was dreaming or hallucinating—pursed a pair of pouty, full pink lips. "Hmm. If you say so." He grinned, showing even white teeth, and despite his fear, Ben swooned. *Goddamn, the man is gorgeous.*

"I'm dreaming, aren't I?" He nodded, confident he was right. "Yep. This is certainly a dream. A good one, of course. I mean, you're someone I'd fantasize about in a dream, so that's always a good sign." Relief swelled through his chest. "I'm going to go back to bed now. I'll probably jerk off, so don't take offence." He laughed uncertainly. "Right, this is me, going back to bed."

He turned away from the apparition and strode back to his bedroom. Once he got there, he climbed into bed, muttered at Tess for not doing her bodyguard duty, pulled the covers up to his chin, and closed his eyes.

The image of the dream man remained etched on his retinas, and Ben's hard-on showed no signs of diminishing. Perhaps it was time to take himself in hand and rub one out. It would help him get back to sleep.

He reached down to caress his aching dick and groaned softly as his strokes grew firmer. Now, this was more like it.

"Need a hand with that?"

Ben yelled and sat bolt upright in bed, holding the duvet in front of him like a shield. He reached over and turned on the bedside lamp. "What the fuck?" he asked for the second time that night.

Seated in the corner of the room was the being from Ben's dream. His legs were draped over the arm of the chair, and he looked thoroughly at ease. He waved an elegant hand at Ben.

"Hi-i," he drawled sexily. "Would you like me to join you and take care of your problem? I figured you enjoy men's company seeing as how you said you dream about them." He winked.

"How?" Ben asked dazedly. "You aren't really here."

By now, Tess had wakened sleepily and was eyeing the apparition with interest. She didn't seem bothered to see an uninvited, half-naked man in Ben's home. Granted, he admitted to himself, she'd seen a few of them from time to time when he'd had a hook-up.

The man stood up, the scent of something soft and spicy wafting from him, tantalising Ben's nostrils. "I beg to disagree. I am certainly here because *you* called me." He sat down next to Ben on the bed. "Let me elucidate. The lamp chose you. You rubbed the lamp. I am the Djinn of the lamp. Ergo, I come when you call." He smirked. "At other times, it truly depends on how good you are with that thing." He glanced appreciatively at Ben's groin.

Ben shook his head. "I have a genie in my bedroom? The sort that grants wishes and shit?" He preferred the modern version of the word because the other one sounded like the popular alcoholic spirit.

The sexy intruder nodded his head. "Give the man a slice of mango. He gets it. My name is Daeliel Jadu Alario, son of Medeaus and Sameria of Quimaria, and I am currently the Keeper Of Cal'dor. Until I can find some way to get out of it permanently, that is." His face darkened with his last words and his lips twisted into a sneer. "I am honour-bound under the Rules of the Accord to be your guide into the world of wishes." He grinned wolfishly. "Be careful how you ask for them. I've had people beg me to take their wish back, but alas, once it's granted, there is no return." The genie bowed. "To whom might I have the pleasure of addressing?"

"My name's Ben. Ben Sinclair."

"Nice to meet you, Ben."

Ben closed his eyes, and when he opened them, the apparition was still there. He decided to humour the man. "So…these wishes. Can I ask for *anything*? And why did you say the lamp chose me?"

Daeliel cocked his head. "Let me give you the sales spiel, then that'll be out of the way." He began ticking things off on his long, lean fingers, and Ben only then noticed his nails were painted a shimmery black. "A Djinn cannot grant eternal life. We cannot heal anyone or anything from sickness or accident. I cannot bring back the dead. We can't make someone love someone else. We cannot change body parts—I've been asked *soooo* many times to make dicks and boobs bigger, and vaginas tighter, but alas," he shrugged, "I don't do that." His eyes lasciviously slid down Ben's body. "Not that I think you have any problems in that area."

Ben preened a little. It was his dream—he was sticking to that concept because, damn it, the alternative was insane—and he could take the accolades if he wanted to.

The genie continued. "I can't fix anything emotional, that's up to the human. We don't meddle in what goes on in your brains because," he grimaced, "who'd want to be in the mire of what you people call your psyche? It's simply far too messy." He stopped. His forehead scrunched. "I think that's about it. Clearer now? Oh, and the lamp doesn't appear to *anyone*. It decides who it goes to."

Ben was still caught up in the wish thing. "What if I say something without thinking, like, I wish it would rain? Would that be a wish?" He frowned thoughtfully. "I'd hate to waste one."

Daeliel rolled his eyes. "No, we have safeguards against that kind of thing happening. Back in the days when we were still fairly new at this thing, one of my forebears had to produce a whole menagerie of elephants with wings for some fool, and the shitstorm that rained down from the skies was worse than one of the plagues of Egypt." He shuddered and so did Ben, imagining huge pats of foul-smelling elephant poop falling from above. "So now a person has to say first, 'Oh Djinn of the lamp, please grant me my wish' and then proceed to tell me what they desire."

Ben nodded sagely. His dream guy was sensible. He approved. "Oh, well, that sounds easy enough. Do I get three wishes then?"

Tess snuffled and lay back down to sleep, crowding Ben as she did, taking up most of the bed.

Daeliel's beautiful face tensed. "That's an urban legend caused by your culture of misappropriating the Djinn community and twisting it to your ends. You get *two* wishes. That's it. A Djinn *may* approve a third one, but that's only done in extreme circumstances." He sniffed haughtily. "I've never found a human being worth granting the third wish yet. I have no doubt you'll be of the same ilk."

"Wow, that's a bit harsh," Ben stated, leaning forward, waving an arm. The bedcover fell away, revealing more of him. Daeliel didn't seem to mind, given the narrowing of his eyes and the slide of a pink tongue across his lips. "You don't even know me."

Daeliel snorted. "Please. I've been around three hundred years in human terms, lived through the Boer War, famines, floods, the rise of the Cold War, and Chernobyl. You humans haven't yet once disabused me of my convictions. The eternal aim for each one of you is the premise of *me, me, me.*" His purplish eyes darkened. "You can't imagine what I've seen."

Ben leaned back against the headboard. "I understand there are some bad people out there. I'm one of those who likes to believe the best in people. Look at Pasteur, Mother Theresa, Christian Barnard, and those who developed vaccines for fatal diseases. What about all those people who lost their lives saving others, as they did in nine-eleven."

Daeliel didn't look convinced. One eyebrow raised haughtily.

"Oh, and Elvis Presley," Ben garbled. "I mean, come on. The man was a legend."

Daeliel looked at him in pity. "Have you ever gone onto Wikipedia and Googled 'history of the past three hundred years'? Take a look at the time line. There may be one or two snippets of good news in there, but overall, it looks like a fucking disaster zone for the ages."

The Djinn stood up and stretched, allowing Ben a glimpse of his taut stomach, a fine line of dark hair leading into his slinky pants. "Forgive me if I seem disillusioned. It's because I am." The last words were said bitterly, and the sassy man Ben was starting to like evolved into a darker version.

"Well, I suppose if you're as old as you say, you have seen some of the worst the world has to offer." Ben pulled the bed cover farther up his chest, feeling rather vulnerable under the genie's piercing purple gaze. "So, what happens now? I go back to sleep, and you'll be gone in the morning?" He snuggled down best he could with the space Tess had left him.

Daeliel flapped a hand. "Whatever. You are a hard man to convince, aren't you?" He stretched, a lithe, fluid movement that made Ben's mouth dry up. "Do you have a spare bedroom? I suppose I should make myself at home." He sniffed. "I hope it's large enough for all my stuff."

"Your stuff?" Ben said. "What stuff?" He looked around the room but didn't see anything lurking.

Daeliel huffed. "You'll see. Now, where's my room?"

Ben blinked. He supposed he'd play along with his dream a little longer. "It's next door to mine. I use it for storage, but there's a bed in there, and some other stuff. You might have to move it around a bit." There was a bed in there *somewhere,* he knew. The room had become something of a dumping ground for spare lab equipment, textbooks, posters, small animal cages, and myriad other crap he'd collected over the years.

The Djinn regarded him uncertainly. "I'm not particularly encouraged by the way you said that." He rolled his eyes. "Never matter. I'll have it all sorted soon enough." He turned, and Ben had a marvellous view of a pert backside and strong thighs. But the item that caught his attention most was the intricate tattoo curling up from beneath Daeliel's low-slung trousers, across his back and spreading across his shoulders. It was an intricate lacing of thin branches winding around a central tree trunk. The colours of dark blue, grey, and black entwined to form an intriguing expanse of mystery across a smooth, tanned back. Ben thought he spied a large black bird—a raven, perhaps—perched on one of the branches.

"Your tattoo is incredible," he murmured. "It looks so authentic and beautifully rendered."

Daeliel turned and regarded him with hooded eyes. "The curse of the Djinn lives on me, and inside me. It is a thing I'd gladly relinquish."

The genie walked out the door, and in Ben's last glimpse of that enticing back, he was sure the raven had moved some branches.

Chapter 4

Ben woke to the sound of soft chanting, and once again, there were bloody chimes, but different from last night. *Must be in the lane outside.* He scowled. Had the local home store had a damned special on them, or what? It was only seven on a Saturday morning, and whoever was playing with them was an inconsiderate wanker.

He grunted and pulled his pillow over his head. Tess snored on beside him. "It's not enough to have horses' hooves, tractors, and bloody chatty cyclists passing by, now I've got some sort of Hare Krishna group outside?" he muttered. The chanting grew louder, and Ben frowned. It didn't sound as if it were coming from outside, after all. It sounded suspiciously like someone was in the house. Downstairs in the lounge to be exact.

Unease meandered up Ben's spine and laid insidious eggs in his brain. Surely that sexy guy from last night had been a dream, and he wasn't still here. No, that couldn't be. Ben must have left the TV on, and there was some sort of morning exercise routine going on.

He heaved a sigh of relief. That was it. Problem solved. He snuggled back into his duvet with a sigh. The chanting grew louder, and suddenly there was a loud crash.

"Frozen Satan on a flying pig," a familiar voice shouted out on a snarl.

Ben couldn't take it anymore. He bolted out of bed, pulled on his joggers—this time he wasn't going to be showing all his bits—and dashed down the narrow stairs into the lounge. The sight that met his eyes was one he never could've imagined.

Daeliel lay, crumpled on the floor, his long legs twisted in a fashion Ben didn't think was possible. He was overwhelmed by three facts.

1) Daeliel was still here.

2) He wore nothing but a tight pair of white, near see-through yoga pants.

3) A vase Ben had hated, but treasured for many years was now lying in several large pieces on the floor.

He moved over and picked up the bits. "What on earth did you do? And why the hell are you still here?"

Daeliel straightened himself out, puffing with exertion, then glared at Ben. "What part of 'Hello. I'm a Djinn here to grant you two wishes' do you not understand, you moronic son of a beaver? Until I grant you your wishes, I'm here to stay."

Ben could only gape at Daeliel as he sprung off the yoga mat in one graceful move and reached for a small towel lying on the couch. The Djinn wiped the sweat from his face and flung the towel back down.

"Some clueless animal was making an infernal racket this morning, and I had no option but to leave my bed," Daliel said waspishly. "You should shoot the damned thing." He waved outside. "I saw it on the fence over there."

Ben blinked at the thought of getting rid of Tricky Dicky. Christine would kill him if he did. She adored her rooster.

"That's not happening," he mumbled. Ben sank into the armchair and passed a hand across his eyes. "You were supposed to be a dream. Are you telling me this is all real?"

Daeliel picked up a bottle of water—Ben noticed it was the brand he bought, so it had come from his fridge—and drank thirstily. Despite his panic at being caught in a fairy tale, he still had the stones to admire the movement of Daeliel's Adam's apple as he chugged down the water, and the way a few stray drops lingered on his chin, then coyly dropped onto his hairless chest to linger there. Ben had never wanted to lick the water off someone as much as he did right now.

Setting the bottle down, Daeliel sighed. "A thousand times, yes. That's my purpose. What you need to do is make those wishes quickly, and I can get back to my world." He looked at Ben hopefully. "Do you want one of those wishes to be fixing that awful object you're holding in your hands? Because I can do that. Then there's only one more, and I can be on my way."

Ben stared down sadly at the pieces in his hand. "This is a Clarice Cliff Newport pottery vase left to me by my mother when she died. Yes, it's hideous, but it was hers."

Daeliel blinked. "Your mother died? How awful. I'm so sorry."

He sounded genuinely sympathetic, and Ben shrugged. "It was a long time ago. I was twenty-two. I don't have much left to remind me of her."

Daeliel came over to crouch before him. "I was trying to do a headstand scorpion, I have trouble with that yoga pose, and I lost my balance. My foot caught the vase on the table and, well, it fell off. I'm truly mortified." He stood up swiftly, his crotch now alarmingly close to Ben's line of sight. "Let me see what I can do. I *suppose* it isn't fair to expect you to use one of your wishes when I'm the one who broke it." He sounded surprised at his words, and Ben guessed that using one of *his* wishes would have suited his desire to hasten Daeliel's path home.

The Djinn closed his eyes and seemed to be in a trance. His lips moved as if he were reciting something under his breath. A faint aura of pale lavender surrounded him, tendrils flicking out into the air and then being almost sucked back in. It was most unsettling. As was the fact Daeliel's junk was enticingly close.

"It doesn't matter." Ben cleared his throat. "I can superglue it together."

Daeliel went still, then opened one eye. "Superglue?"

Ben nodded. "Yeah. I can stick the pieces with it, so it's whole again. It won't be the same, but meh, it's the memory that counts, right?"

Daeliel beamed at him and the lavender aura dissipated. "Splendid. I searched the annals for any precedence to giving a wish for free, and it can be done, but of course, it is frowned upon. Best not to annoy the authorities if we don't have to." He patted Ben on the shoulder and turned away. "I think I've done enough damage for one day. I'd better get changed." He picked up his mat, rolled it up, and then headed towards the stairs.

Ben followed Daeliel, feeling distinctly out of sorts, and entered the spare bedroom after him. Once again, his senses were assaulted with something which surely couldn't be. He stopped and stared in amazement at the kaleidoscope of colour and mayhem before him.

"How the fuck is this possible?" he muttered dazedly. "You couldn't possibly have been shopping for all this stuff already."

His spare bedroom, once a neutral shade of beige and brown, now resembled a room Ben had once seen at Alton Towers. He'd been there helping out with an animal in distress and been given a tour of the top floor and the suites. This room resembled the Arabian Nights one, although with more colour and a sense of style more suited to a showgirl's dressing room.

Daeliel smirked as he put his thumbs into the waistband of his pants and pulled them down to reveal a pert backside and more of the tattoo that had captured Ben's imagination the night before. "Do you forget who I am and what I can do?"

Ben averted his gaze, although it took a lot of effort. "Whoa, dude. Not cool." *Way cool. If it were any cooler, I'd be a dicksicle.* "Don't you have privacy requirements where you come from?"

Daeliel paused in the process of pulling on a skin-tight pair of pale blue chinos. No underwear, Ben thought with a gulp. He's commando under those.

"Privacy? Don't you like looking at me?" Daeliel sounded piqued. "Where I come from, bodies are made to be displayed and explored. Don't you find mine to your liking?"

Ben swallowed. "I, um, like it, um, very much. It's, well, um, here in this world, we're sort of more, um, uptight about showing our private bits to just anyone. We're British. We're not as open about expressing our sexuality as you seem to be."

Daeliel scoffed as he picked up a filmy indigo shirt with a Chinese collar trimmed with gold. "Ah, yes. The human traits of coyness and denial. I'd forgotten. It's been a while since I was in your world." He pulled the shirt over his head, and it moulded like silk to his tanned skin. "I find that a little tedious. I tend to take my kit off any chance I get." The wicked smile Daeliel threw Ben's way was incendiary, and threatened to ignite Ben's underwear given the heat in his groin.

The Djinn waved a hand around the room. "Do you like it? I got myself a few creature comforts and conjured up a liveable place to spend my time in this world. I may be forced to be here, but the least I can do is make it a home from home, yes?"

"It's very *you*," Ben admitted. "From the little I know of you, anyway. Is this what your room on your home planet looks like?"

Daeliel made an irritated sound. "Oh, friscuit. Another one who talks like a sci-fi nerd." He said disparagingly. "I don't come from another *planet*. I come from another realm, outside this one. I am not a Dr Who contender, nor do I have anything to do with that tiresome show you call *Star Trek*."

Ben's temper flared. "I'm sorry, but this is all new to me. Are you always such a condescending git?"

Daeliel's eyes widened, a look of surprise crossing his face. "You're angry with me?" He didn't sound as if that happened often.

"You're an arsehole. I've never had a genie make a home in my house before so forgive me if I ask stupid questions."

Daeliel pursed his lips. "Still you use that new-fangled terminology." He snapped his mouth shut, no doubt because Ben moving closer to him was a warning sign. "I mean, if I have offended you, I'm sorry."

Ben stopped and gestured to the room. "Forget it. How did you manage to get this room to look like this in such a short time?"

Daeliel blinked. "I'm a Djinn. I can create environments and scenarios to fit my surroundings."

Ben felt like he was fighting a losing battle. "Yes, but where's *my* furniture and where did *yours* come from?"

The Djinn's face cleared. "Ah, I see. Well, I simply opened an ethereal portal to my realm and rented a storage locker for your stuff. I then took mine out of storage and voila." He waved around the room again.

"You rented an outer realm storage locker?" Ben asked, his voice strangled. "How does that even fucking happen?"

Daeliel frowned. "I paid a deposit, filled in a form and—"

Ben was ready to blow in frustration. "Oh my God. You are the most annoying individual I've ever met, and I've met a few." He took a deep breath. "I'm less concerned with what you did to rent the damned locker, but more the how. How the hell does it all work?"

Daeliel didn't say anything. He huffed and made a strange gesture with his fingers. The air around them grew heavy, dull, almost like the aftermath of an explosion, when everything was muted. The colours in the room grew dim, and something strange formed in front of them. Ben likened it to a cloud, fluffy and transparent. He gasped when he saw the familiar shape of his old bed and the shabby chest of drawers.

"Would you like me to bring it back?" Daeliel asked with a polite sneer. "If you're that partial to it all…" He waggled his fingers, and to Ben's amazement, the bed began to move closer, making its way to the entrance of the portal. Ben had visions of a *Bedknobs and Broomsticks* scenario, and replied hastily, "No, leave it there. I only wanted to see how you did it."

I can't believe I'm having this conversation. I must still be dreaming.

To make sure, he did what all people did when they were trying to see whether they were dreaming or not. He pinched himself. Harder than he'd intended because he yowled.

"Ow." He gazed around him in a daze. "I guess I *am* awake. Holy crap."

Daeliel threw him a shade-filled glance and looked around the room. "Let me do another little trick to convince you." His lip curled and with a flick of his fingers, a large, ornate hand mirror lifted off the dressing table next to Ben and floated past him, into the portal, to land on the bed on the other side.

"I have another one of those," Daeliel muttered. He made a circling motion with his fingers, and the portal closed. Ben stood there in astonishment.

"That's how it works," the Djinn decreed. "I still have magic, even here, simply not as powerful. Happy now?"

"Huh," Ben grunted. His mind was blown, and he needed a stiff drink. "Going back to something you said earlier. You've been here in this world before?"

Daeliel nodded. "Yes, I was last here three earth years ago. A young lady brought me forth. I granted her wishes and left. She was *extremely* accommodating in asking for her wishes speedily, allowing me to get back to my world." He emphasised the last sentence.

"What did she wish for?" Ben asked curiously.

Daeliel wagged a finger. "I'm afraid I can't say. Djinn/Wisher confidentiality and all that." He smiled wickedly. "Suffice it to say, she's a big Hollywood star, so her wishes certainly came true." He made a moue. "Who knew a film about abduction and other depressing human subjects would be so iconic?"

"What happens when you grant the person their wishes?" Ben leaned against the doorjamb. "Do you, uhm, go back into the lamp straight away?"

Daeliel nodded. "Once their wishes have been granted, I go back to Calodo'r. That's the lamp's true name."

"Do you like it there? What's it like?" Ben watched as Daeliel's face clouded.

"It's got nothing to do with what I like. It's my duty to be there, so there I am. It's a beautiful place, and I suppose I'm contented enough." Daeliel's tone grew sharp. "Anyway, enough of me. Have you given any consideration to what you'd like to wish for?"

Ben shook his head. "No. I'm still not sure this is real. It'll take me some time to get my head around all this." He waved a hand. "I don't want to waste my wishes. I want to be sure about what I ask for."

Daeliel heaved a sigh. "Very well. I shall make myself comfortable for a while and give you more time." He sat down on the bed and pushed his feet into a pair of elegant loafers. "I shall go for a walk, familiarise myself with your world once again. It'll be good to see what's changed."

"That's cool," Ben said. "I've got to be at work for my shift by ten anyway, so…do you need a key or something, to get back in the house?"

I can't believe I'm having this conversation. Maybe I'm hallucinating, and this is still a dream.

Deep inside, Ben knew he was awake, and yes, he had asked a magical genie if he wanted a front door key to come and go as he pleased.

"Oh Ben, that's adorable." Daeliel stood up, reached out and caressed Ben's cheek. "Thinking I need a key. I suppose I should have one to create a semblance of normality." His brow furrowed. "What kind of work do you do?"

"I'm a zoologist at the local zoo. I also look out for the penguins. It's a small zoo, so we all tend to get involved in more than one function."

"Oh, a learned man and an animal lover. You've become *much* more interesting." Daeliel winked. "I shall have to visit this zoo of yours." He pursed his lips. "I noticed you have another little critter in your living room other than the large dog on your bed. It looks almost dead, did you know that?"

Ben chuckled. "No, that's my guinea pig. He's old, so he doesn't move around much." Ben made a mental note to double-check Pookums was still breathing.

"Ah. I look forward to meeting him later. Anyway, let me get out of your way so you can get ready for work. I'll see you later, no doubt." Daeliel disappeared out of the room.

Ben looked around him. *This is truly happening. A genie has visited me. Now all I have to do is make those wishes and life will get back to normal.*

As he wandered into the bathroom to take a shower, Ben's mind buzzed with the possibilities.

Seems like all those stories Mom told me about otherworldly creatures were true after all.

Chapter 5

Daeliel strolled down the tree-lined lane, spying a bunch of almost ripe blackberries growing in the hedgerow. He shuffled over to pick a couple, popping them in his mouth. They were sweet and juicy with a distinct tart flavour. From behind the bushes, a few bored sheep stared at him, then turned back to grazing.

This morning, he'd lain down on his bed and fallen asleep again. His nightmares had been hazy, but real, and when he'd woken up from his uneasy sleep, Ben was gone, and Tess was lying on his bed. No matter what he'd done to shoo her off, she'd regarded him with big brown eyes, and after a while, he'd given up trying to move her. Instead, he'd gotten up, and dressed and decided to check out the neighbourhood the old-fashioned way.

He'd rather be up anyway. The air was a little chilly, and Daeliel's shirt didn't afford him much warmth, but he quite enjoyed the feel of the cool fabric against his skin.

This world hasn't changed much, he reflected as he walked. It was quite different from the last time he'd been here when he'd landed in London. He wasn't in the city now, but he doubted much had changed there. Perhaps there would be new buildings and a more cosmopolitan look to the pavements with the variety of people crossing each other's path, but underneath, it would still be the same city. Diverse, energetic, and a pleasing mix of old and new.

Daeliel, however, *was* intrigued by Ben Sinclair. The man was a veritable taste-fest with his stubbled chin and swathe of artfully styled hair. And those deep blue eyes? Enticing. They contributed to the overall package of Ben's clean-cut cheekbones and strong jawline. Not to forget, the glimpse Daeliel'd had of the man in full frontal mode had been a sight to make a Djinn's mouth water.

"I'm not so sure I *want* to leave too quickly," he murmured to a horse as he passed. The animal carried on munching grass. "As much as I want to get back, I feel he could prove a welcome distraction for a while." Daeliel's face darkened as he considered going back. Calado'r had only been his residence for the past five years—fifty in human time—and it hadn't been his choice to be there in the first place.

He refused to call it home. His throat tightened as he thought of Aether and his parents—and of course, the banishing. Daeliel had considered himself past the point of feeling as if his heart was ripped out of his chest, with the accompanying anguish at the thought of Aether's betrayal.

I still don't know how you could have done that to me. You destroyed my world. You destroyed us.

As he'd done so many times before, Daeliel pushed his pain deep down into his secret place. This was not the time to linger on a tragedy which should stay buried.

His journey home a few hours later was sombre. He'd been intrigued by many things on his walk, including some old ruins he'd delighted in exploring, which had brought back memories of him and Aether together, stealing away for forbidden kisses.

His good mood evaporated with the thoughts of the past. By the time he pushed his key into the lock—the human use of it *did* make him smile since he could apparate where he wanted at will—his only greeting was a small animal lying on the inside front doormat.

He stared down at it in confusion. The little creature didn't move, and Daeliel had a feeling he knew why. He reached down and prodded it with a wary finger. The animal was cool and covered in dirt, its eyes closed. It looked peaceful, but Daeliel knew what death looked like.

It resembled the one he'd seen in the cage in the lounge. A guinea pig, he thought Ben had said. But how had it gotten out and why was it now here, deceased?

"Poor thing," he murmured, pressing his forefinger to the little furry head, and saying a short invocation to speed the creature's soul onto better things. Tess trotted in through the open patio door, sat down beside him and looked up, tail wagging. Her muzzle was covered in dirt.

Daeliel swore. His eyes widened. "Did you do this, you horrible beast? You should be ashamed of yourself." He leaned down and plucked the unfortunate animal from the floor. Tess looked up at him, tongue lolling out of the side of her mouth, not looking particularly guilty. For a dog, she sure had some human expressions.

"Ben is going to be devastated when he comes home and sees what you've done, you murderer, you." He took the dirty, stiffening guinea pig into the bathroom. He supposed he could clean it up, put it back in the cage and Ben would be none the wiser for a while. Of course, he'd be devastated once he discovered his pet was deceased, but that couldn't be helped.

Even a Djinn couldn't bring the dead back to life.

Twenty minutes and a half bottle of apple-scented shampoo (the dratted animal had been dirtier than he thought) later, the creature had been placed back in its cage in the corner of the living room. Daeliel preened as he surveyed his handiwork. He hadn't quite been able to make the creature look as if it was comfortable, as its little limbs had been quite uncooperative, but at least it looked as if it was sleeping on its side.

"I think I've saved your bacon, missy," he scolded the dog as he settled in to watch television and catch up on world events. This modern world could be quite entertaining when it needed to be.

***

It was around six when the front door opened. Ben shouted, "Dae, I'm home." There was a clatter as he chucked something large onto the dining table. Daeliel winced. He'd polished it to a shine this afternoon and made faces at himself in the sheen of the wood.

I hope the buffoon hasn't scuffed it.

Ben walked into the lounge, looking tired and a little pissed off. Tess got up and ambled over to him. He patted her head and scratched behind her ears. She closed her eyes in pleasure.

"You look as if you had a rough day. Are you all right?" Dae queried.

"Yeah, I'm good. One of my penguins got injured today, and we had to do some emergency surgery on her." Ben walked over to the pet cage and stared down at it sadly. Dae held his breath as he cast a glance at Tess, who lay down watching Ben adoringly.

"Oh no. Is she okay?" Dae switched off the telly.

Ben nodded tiredly. "Yes, she's fine. Some dickhead threw a plastic beer can holder into the water. Daisy got her beak caught and hurt herself trying to get it off."

Daeliel thought it was cute the way Ben gave his birds names.

"What the holy fuck?" Ben exclaimed as he leaned towards the cage.

Daeliel strolled over and peered innocently into it too. "What's wrong?"

"That." Ben pointed to the cage, his eyes rounded in shock. "What the hell is he doing in there?"

Daeliel frowned. "What do you mean?"

"I mean, what the fuck is he doing in the cage?"

Daeliel wasn't quite sure where this was heading, but he sensed something wasn't going quite the way he'd planned it. He chose levity and a patronising attitude to help him through it.

"Well, unless he's grown opposable thumbs and can open the door himself, where else would he be?"

Ben's face darkened. "Pookums died in the night. I noticed this morning when I came to check on him before I went to work. I buried him out in the garden. So how the fuck did he get back in here?" His face brightened. "Unless you had something to do with this. Did you bring him back to life? You said you couldn't do that. Actually, I wouldn't want you to anyway, given what happened in *Pet Sematary*." A visible shudder ran through his body. "If you can, I'm not sure that's wise, considering how that turned out for everyone."

Daeliel blinked. He had no idea what Ben was talking about but made a mental note to Google it later. It sounded—entertaining.

"Oh, you think it's dead?" he said. He reached into the cage with his long finger and prodded it. "Hmm. It does seem rather unresponsive. It must have had a heart attack or something. Poor thing."

"He died of old age," Ben said between gritted teeth. "My original question stands. How did he find his way out of the garden grave I dug and into here?" He leaned in and sniffed. "Why does he smell of apples?"

Daeliel glared at Tess, who he was sure was grinning a blue streak at his predicament. *Just you wait*, he promised, hoping she could hear him. *I am so going to get you for this one.*

Wait a minute—Pookums? He snickered.

"So?" Ben demanded.

Daeliel sighed. "It appears I have been fooled. I found the little creature on the doormat when I got home. I thought he'd gotten out the cage and the beast here had killed him. It appears now she must have dug him up and brought him inside."

"You thought you'd put him back in the cage? Why?" Ben's perplexed look was epic.

"I thought you would be mad at her for killing him, so best I put him back in the cage and allow you to think he died naturally," Daeliel said stiffly. "I, er, washed him before I did so."

"You washed a dead guinea pig and put it back in its cage, so I didn't get angry," Ben said dazedly. "Wow. I don't even know what to say to that."

He looked from Tess to Daeliel, and his shoulders began to shake. At first, Daeliel thought he was crying. When Ben looked up again, the tears on his face fell in laughter, not grief.

"This is surreal. Oh my god. It's too funny, no disrespect, Pookums, but if you were still here, you'd be chuckling too." He went off in another hooting bout of merriment.

"I don't think guinea pigs chuckle." Daeliel scowled. Really, who knew what humans would do next? They were such unpredictable creatures. "However, I'm glad you find my lapse in judgment amusing."

Ben wiped his eyes and rubbed his nose. "Sorry, but you have to admit, it's hella funny." His face softened. "Honestly? I think what you did was sweet, trying to protect Tess." He nudged Daeliel's arm with his elbow. "Seems you have quite the soft side to you."

Daeliel sniffed. "I did what I thought was right." As he said the words, echoes of Aether saying the same thing drifted into his memory. He forced them out. "Would you like me to redress my action?"

Ben looked at him with a frown. "What *exactly* does that mean?" He opened the cage and reached inside, picking Pookums up gently and cradling the little body in his hands. "If you mean do I want to put him back where he should be, I'll do it." The reverence with which Ben treated his pet almost brought a lump to Daeliel's throat. He swallowed to make it go away.

Ben walked toward the open back door and the garden. "I'll lay him to rest—again—and then we can discuss what we're having for dinner. I thought perhaps we'd order in some Chinese?"

"That would be fine," Daeliel said, his mouth watering at the thought of a little garlic shrimp and some soy sauce noodles.

Ben nodded and disappeared into the darkening evening.

***

"As you're my guest, tell me about yourself," Ben mumbled as he shovelled another mouthful of delicious moo shoo pork into his mouth. Across from him, Dae sat, enjoying his tasty dish. "I think I need to know more about the man staying at my house."

A man who looked exceptionally handsome tonight.

Daliel was dressed in a midnight blue tight silky tee-shirt and a pair of black jeans that moulded to his every curve. His straight hair hung around his sexy cheekbones and strong jaw, giving him the striking look of a regal prince. Ben could see him cast as such in a Disney film. He knew *he'd* drool over the character.

Ben's dreams last night included sexy versions of him and his gorgeous houseguest getting up to more than friendship. And why not? The man was attractive, intelligent, and fun. His tight bum was a delight to behold, together with rosy, kissable lips.

Dae swallowed what he was chewing and looked over at him cagily with his hypnotising dark purple eyes. "I've told you everything you need to know," he muttered, then picked up another shrimp. "I'm not sure what else there is."

"Are you kidding me?" Ben laid his fork down. "You've lived hundreds of years, came out of a damn brass lamp, and taken over my home. I'm fairly sure you have a lot to tell me. Like, do you have family, what's it like in the lamp, and how does it all work?"

Dae stiffened, an expression of caution crossing his strong features. "I'm here to grant you wishes—which I hope you'll do soon, by the way—not pander to your curiosity." He pushed his forkful of food into his mouth with a little more force than was necessary.

I've hit a tender spot. He's edgy about something I've asked.

Ben shrugged. "Fair enough. You don't want to talk. No need to be rude."

Dae heaved an irritated sigh and put down his fork. "I didn't mean to be. It's only that family and my past is a bit of a sore subject. I'd rather not talk about it."

"Okay." Ben took a sip of his beer. He tried hard to respect Dae's wishes, but it simply wasn't possible. His mother had told him often he had the curiosity of a meerkat. "So at least tell me what life in the lamp is like? I bet it's an exciting place."

"By Beza's Beard, you don't give up, do you?" Dae thwacked his hand.

Ben chuckled. "I like your weird expressions. They're cool."

The genie rolled his eyes. "Fine, I'll tell you a little." He took a deep breath. "Calado'r is a beautiful place. It's a bit like—" His face squinched up in an adorable frown. "I suppose like your world's version of the film *Aladdin*. You almost got it right. Not quite, though." He waved a hand. "We have the sea, beautiful mountains, deserts and forests, and cities of all kinds. There are all kinds of people in Calado'r."

"Were you born there?" Ben leaned in, fascinated. He was enjoying the scent of Daeliel, a sandalwood and spice fragrance alluring to the senses.

Dae's face darkened. "No. I am not a true Calodo'rean." He hesitated. "I'm from the Fae kingdom of Quimaria. I am Faerie born."

Ben gaped. "Shouldn't you have wings?" He regretted the words the minute they left his mouth.

Dae's face shuttered closed, and he stood up swiftly. "Not all Fae have wings. I think that's enough. I have things to do. Have you thought of a wish yet?"

The abrupt turnaround in conversation left Ben a little out of sorts. "I've thought about it, but not yet decided on making one."

"Make one. Then make another one. It's the only way I can go back." Dae turned and swept out of the room.

Huh. That didn't go as well as I'd planned.

If Ben was trapped in this strange relationship, the least he wanted was for both of them to bond, if only a little. He sighed and slumped down on the couch.

Perhaps he could find a documentary somewhere on Djinns and get to know Dae a little better that way.

Chapter 6

"That's it, Sammy," Ben cajoled as he swam through the seal pool with his arm around a small baby seal. "You can do it, look at you, you're nearly swimming on your own."

It was late evening, the zoo was closed, and Sammy was having his swimming lesson. The young South American fur pup had lost his mother at birth. Because the pup had no mother to teach him how to swim, Ben had been nominated.

It was no hardship. Ben loved being in the water, and diving was a regular part of his job. Sometimes it was for fun, playing with the penguins and seals, and other times it was for a more serious reason, like today.

He laughed as Sammy grew bolder and swam away on his own to fetch a bobbing ball floating on the surface. The seal nudged it with his nose and pushed it towards Ben.

"You want me to throw it?" Ben asked as he plucked it from the water and tossed it gently, careful not to throw too high. "Here you go. We're nearly done here. Then it's time for your dinner." Being only eight weeks old with no mother, Sammy had been reared on fish milkshakes. They were as gross as they sounded, but the baby seal loved them.

An hour later, out of his wet suit, freshly showered and ready to go home, all his animals fed and content, Ben popped into the staff room to say his good-byes. Hemingway was there, along with the general manager, Hazel Reyes, a comely Puerto Rican woman who ran the zoo with an iron fist encased in a velvet glove. Most of her team would do anything for a smile from the bubbly dark-haired woman. A compliment from Hazel was a sought-after commodity.

"Ben, my friend." Hemingway waved a cup at him from where he sat on the kitchen counter. "Fancy a drink before you go? I have made a fresh pot of coffee."

"Sure, thanks." Ben smiled at them. A warm drink would heat him up before the cycle ride home. His friend picked up a cup from the draining board and poured a rich-smelling brew into the cup. Ben walked over and took it from him. "Thanks. It's been a long day, and this is welcome." He took a sip and eyed out Hazel. "Hey, boss, I heard a rumour we got a rather large donation today from some huge construction company? Is that true?"

Hazel nodded, her dark eyes sparkling. "We did. I was at a networking event last week and managed to convince them to open their chequebook." She grinned. "The owner of the company has a son who works in the Arctic with snowbirds and is always on at him to donate to animal preservation charities. It wasn't a big stretch to sell us to the cause, and of course, my powers of persuasion can be amazingly effective," she purred. Her face sobered. "It's just as well, because there's so much to do here, and the money will be put to good use. This place sucks money like a leech."

Ben and Hemingway nodded. Ben knew that funding for the zoo was always a challenge. The situation a few months ago had been dire and it was only at the last minute Hazel had secured enough funding to keep them going.

"No shit," Ben murmured. "I bet you charmed the pants off them." He hesitated. Was he about to make a complete fool of himself? "Say, guys, do either of you believe in, like, the supernatural at all?" Even as he said the words, he winced in embarrassment.

Hemingway chortled. "You are talking to an African man brought up in the myths of my ancestors." Ben knew Hemingway was from Botswana. "Of course, I believe in it. The *Tokoloshe*, hooting owls, black cats and *nkisi*—believe me, I've heard them all." He frowned. "Why do you ask?"

Ben floundered then lied. There was no way he could tell anyone the truth about him Airbnb-ing a genie. "Oh, I was talking to a guest at the zoo, and they were telling me they thought their house was haunted. I thought it was interesting, that's all."

Hazel hummed. "Puerto Rico is a pretty superstitious place. *El Chupacabra*, upside down brooms, the *mal de Ojo* or evil eye. Like

Hemingway, I was brought up with all this. I might not believe them all today, but there are still plenty of things I do that go back to my childhood." She shrugged. "You can take the girl out of Puerto Rico, but you can't take Puerto Rico out of the girl."

Ben nodded thoughtfully. "So weird things can happen, and you don't believe that a person is crazy if they think or see something that is out of this world?"

He knew he'd said too much when Hemingway narrowed his eyes and slid off the countertop. "This sounds oddly specific, Ben, my man. Have you seen an alien or perhaps a werewolf or something?"

Ben hooted in forced laughter. *Yes, a half-naked genie appeared in my house and promised me two wishes. He's staying in my spare bedroom and rents an inter-realm storage locker.* God, he'd be transported away in a white van and never seen again. "No, of course not. This person I was talking too was convinced he had a poltergeist. It was crazy listening to him, but he believed it."

"Uh-huh." Hemingway didn't sound convinced. "If you say so. Anyways," he nudged Ben with his elbow. "If you had anything weird going on in your life, you'd tell your best friend about it, right? That's what BFs do."

Ben nodded vigorously. "Of course I would, Hemmy." *Are you fucking crazy? I'm not looking to get locked up.* "Stranger Things, right? We're a team, you and me, like Mike and Will. Dustin and Steve."

Hemingway's eyes lit up. "Yeah. Like them. Reminds me, it's time for a marathon watch of episodes of *Mindhunter*. Maybe I can come over to yours tonight, and we can get some food and sit and binge-watch? I've got the day off tomorrow."

Ben swallowed. *Oh shit. How am I going to explain Dae living with me?* He knew he could fob Hemmy off once, but the man was a pit bull, and he loved Ben's large TV. He'd think nothing of turning up unannounced and letting himself in.

"Sure, but can't stay up too late. Some of us have to work in the morning." He waved a hand. "Oh, and so you know, I've got someone staying with me temporarily. He's a—" Ben winced, "cousin from Scotland. His name's Daniel. He won't be around long, but he needed somewhere to stay."

Hazel stared at him appraisingly. She raised one perfectly manicured finger to her lips and tapped them thoughtfully.

Shit, have I ever told them I don't have any other family other than Dad? I don't think I did.

Hemingway grinned. "Wow, I didn't even know you had a cousin. That's cool, man. The more, the merrier. What's he doing staying with you?"

Ben stalled. "Erm, he's taking some leave, a sabbatical of some sort."

Hazel looked intrigued. "That implies he's some sort of scholar or something. What does he do?"

Shit, this lie is growing out of control. Keep it simple.

"Not a scholar, he's a consultant in the energy field taking some time out from a busy year."

Hazel winked. "Is he single and looking to date? I'm on a strict man diet at the moment, not through choice, and maybe you could introduce us?" She did a little swirl around. "I mean, who wouldn't want to tap this?"

Ben's throat dried up. "Okay, I wasn't expecting that. TMI, Hazel. And, er, no," he babbled. "Dae-Daniel is taken. His boyfriend is a power bodybuilder from Russia, and he's the jealous type." He emphasised boyfriend so Hazel would get the picture.

Fuck where the hell did that come from? A power bodybuilder from Russia?

His boss pouted. "That sucks. Oh well, I guess it's Tinder again for me." She frowned thoughtfully. "Maybe it's time to call back the last guy I was with. He was cute, even if he was into toy voyaging. I'm sure one of my teddy bears went missing after the last time we hooked up." She waved a hand at Ben and Hemingway. "Anyway, it's getting late. Go home, you two. I'll see you on Monday."

Hazel flounced out of the room. Ben and Hemingway stared at each other.

"Toy voyaging?" Ben asked warily. "I don't think I even want to know what that's all about."

Hemingway pursed his lips. "I suddenly have an undeniable urge to find out all about it." He pulled out his phone, and after a minute, he laughed. "It isn't as bad as you think it is, my friend. Take a look."

Ben wasn't so sure, but he looked at the screen anyway. "Seriously? People do this? Send their stuffed toys on holidays to meet other people?"

"Seems so." Hemingway wriggled his eyebrows. "Say, maybe we should join in? You've got that stuffed penguin on your bed, haven't you? Maybe Little Feet wants to go on vay-cation."

Ben flushed. "His name is Peppermint, and no, I'm not sending him anywhere. He was given to me by one of the kids at the zoo. It would be disrespectful not to keep him."

"Oh, you don't need to explain your weird penguin fetish to me, partner." Hemingway winked. "I've seen you in the pool swimming with them, and I have to say, I don't want to know what goes on under the water." He cackled loudly as Ben threw a punch at his arm. "Ow. Am I tickling a nerve there?"

"Shut up," Ben muttered. "I don't why I put up with you."

"Because I bring Chinese with me when I come to visit—talking of which, I'll see you around seven, like usual?" Hemingway picked up his rucksack and swung it over his shoulder.

Ben nodded grumpily. "Yes, that's fine. Make sure you bring Kung Pao chicken and beer. And ice cream. Pistachio or Cookie Crumble."

Hemingway rolled his eyes as he moved over to the door. "I'll remember, oh bossy one." He flashed a smile. "See you later. I look forward to meeting Daniel." He disappeared out the door.

For a second, Ben had forgotten his house guest, and the thought of Hemmy and Daeliel being in the same room was giving him hives.

I'll have to forewarn Dae to be on his best behaviour and not act out. The last thing I need is him revealing who and what he truly is.

***

Dae stared at Ben, who fidgeted under his glare. The pair were seated on the comfy lounge suite at home, each of them sporting a drink. Ben was having a beer, Dae a glass of red wine.

"Let me get this right. You have a friend coming over tonight to watch television, and I'm supposed to be your cousin Daniel? Do I *look* like I could be your cousin? From Scotland? How the hell do you expect me to put on an accent?"

Ben winced. Dae, in his tight blue leggings (he'd been doing yoga) and a figure-moulding dark green tee-shirt, looked more like one of Ben's hook-ups. One Ben would do in a heartbeat. The man exuded sensuality and primal emotion.

"I'm also an energy expert? Exactly what does an energy expert do?" Dae didn't look amused. "I know I'm a powerhouse of sex and mysticism, but I doubt that's the kind of energy he's expecting."

Ben puffed out his cheeks. He hadn't even told Dae about his Russian bodybuilder boyfriend yet. Small steps, he told himself. "I panicked a bit, okay? Can't you do some of your mojo and, you know, make yourself into something else?"

Dae pursed his oh-so-edible lips. "Hmm, my *mojo*? You think I can simply turn it off and on like that?" He smiled, but it didn't quite reach his eyes. "The last time someone asked me to hide who I was, it didn't turn out so well for me. I was banished from my home, my family, and everything I held dear, and ended up in there, alone." He waved at the lamp. "So forgive me if I don't seem too enthusiastic about your suggestion."

Ben sighed wearily. "I understand. I shouldn't be asking you to lie for me. I'm sorry."

Note to self. Try to find out more about him being banished. Sounds like a helluva story.

The Djinn regarded him edgily. "You do know there's a solution to your problem, don't you? Make your two wishes and I'll be gone. Poof. Then you won't have to explain my presence to anyone."

Ben had almost forgotten about his wishes. The past four days he'd enjoyed Daliel's company, and the reason he was there in the first place had escaped him.

"I know that," Ben remarked softly. "I'm not ready to give you my wishes. I haven't figured out what I want yet."

You. I want you. I like having you around. I don't want you to go.

Dae's face gave nothing away. "Then I'm afraid we're at an impasse, Ben." He turned to leave the room. "You can tell your friend I'm indisposed, and I'll stay in my room. That should solve your problem."

He walked out, leaving Ben behind with a gutful of guilt and an overwhelming sense of loss.

Chapter 7

Dae lay back on his bed, surrounded by some of his favourite items from Quimaria. His treasured quilt, a lush, embroidered affair sporting vivid jewel colours was wrapped around his shoulders. It had been a gift from his mother, Sameria, when he'd been banished. "To remind you of home," she'd said, tears shining in her eyes. His favourite cushion, a soft, hand-painted puffy thing, created by his sister, Jannalor, was clutched to his chest. In his hand, he held a leather wallet, carefully crafted by his father. Inside was a small, hand-written note, signed by all three of his family, and saying one day they'd see him again.

They were all precious things reminding him of home and a loving family he hadn't seen in five years. Wouldn't see for another five, until the full length of banishment had been met.

Dae clutched the pillow to his chest as he stared around his room moodily. "Fuck my life. Everyone always wants me to be something I'm not. Well, a pox on them." He scowled down at his cushion. "Who is this guy coming over, anyway? A hookup? Am I going to be listening to the two of them doing the rumba all night while I lie here all alone?" Dae wasn't sure why the idea bothered him so much.

His face brightened. "Perhaps I should go to a bar or something, and find someone to fuck. It's been a while." His face softened dreamily. In the lamp, there was no shortage of nubile and sexy partners to keep him company.

As the Djinn of Calado'r, plenty of playmates were into partying and making him feel good, in the hope that some of his magic would rub off on them. Dae hadn't told them it didn't work that way. He could do magic, sure, but it was the beneficiary of the wishes who channelled most of it once the lamp was rubbed.

Outside the wind blew, and rain slashed against the windows. It was a miserable night; he promptly decided he wasn't going out, not even for a little stimulation. Dae sighed. He didn't want to stay in his room like a naughty boy. He wanted company, and if that meant changing his attire to something boring and respectable, then so be it. He stood up and walked over to the bookcase in the corner of his room. He was sure he'd seen some fashion magazines, which might give him an idea or two as to look ordinary—*bleh*—while instilling a sense of glamour into his outfit.

The *GQ* magazine he picked up was interesting in a variety of ways. Not only did it feature some cracking fashion ideas, but the plethora of gorgeous men gracing the pages made Dae's research project a pleasure.

He tapped a finger against his chin thoughtfully. "Hmm. That should do." Dae murmured a few words under his breath and grinned as the outfit he wore shimmered and changed. He practised on and off, until finally finding something he was satisfied with. Once he was ready, he stood in front of the mirror—a full-length one he'd conjured up—and contemplated his appearance with glee.

"Wicked. No one's going to ignore me in this. Whoever you are coming over to see Ben—eat your heart out."

***

Ben slumped in his armchair, wondering what Dae was doing in his room. He felt bad about forcing his houseguest to make himself scarce, but it was probably the right thing to do. There was no way he could let Hemingway even get a whiff of anything special about Dae. His best friend's bullshit barometer was strong with *the force*, and he'd pick up the smell from far away.

Ben glanced at his watch. Hemmy would be here any minute, being the punctual person he was. It was usually Ben who turned up late to everything. He stood up and walked over to the kitchen, checking that the oven was on low, so the Chinese food could be warmed up. He bet it would be cold by now given the weather outside.

There was a loud blow to the door and a yell. "I come bearing gifts. Let me in."

Ben grinned and pulled the door open. Hemmy stood there, windswept and wet, his puffy parka stuffed unevenly with cardboard boxes. In his right hand, he held a six-pack of beer. In his left was the promised pistachio ice cream.

Ben stepped back to let him in. "Hurry up. You're letting the rain in."

Hemmy bumbled in, and Ben shut the door quickly. "Get your jacket off, and I'll warm the food in the oven for a minute." He took the beers and the ice cream Hemmy thrust at him and walked into the kitchen. Tess gave a pleased woof and came over for her head to be scratched.

Behind him, his friend heaved a sigh of relief as he took out the food under his jacket. Ben was a little put off seeing his cherished kung pao chicken being plucked from under Hemmy's armpit as he removed his jacket and shoes.

"It shouldn't be too cold given I have been heating it with my body warmth," Hemmy announced. "Take that look off your face. I showered before I came here, and the food is in a sealed box. I bought enough for three of us."

"Still," Ben grumbled as he took the items offered and placed them on the top shelf of the oven. "It's an armpit, Hem. Probably gonna smell of sweat now."

Hemmy smiled widely. "Additional fragrance," he chuckled. "If you think anyone could sweat in that weather out there, you are very much mistaken." He looked around as he took a beer from the six-pack and sauntered over to the couch. "Where's your mystery guest?"

Ben shrugged as he closed the oven and turned to his friend. "Feeling a bit under the weather," he said, guilt washing over him. "He's asleep, I think."

He took himself and his beer over to his armchair and sat down. Hemmy followed, making himself comfortable on the couch and bringing his long legs up to perch on the armrest. His socks were holey and mismatched, one blue, one a bright green.

"That's a pity," his friend countered as he took a swig of his beer. "I was looking forward to meeting him."

"And meet him you shall," a soft, Scots-accented voice said.

Ben swung around to the source of the voice and his jaw dropped. *Holy hotness.* The man looked wicked.

Dae was dressed in a pair of white jeans, which moulded to his long legs. Topped with a white polo-neck, and teamed with a casual waffled dove-grey waistcoat, loosely buttoned at the front, he looked like a GQ model.

In fact...Ben frowned. I *think I've seen that outfit in my GQ magazine. I remember because it was pretty sexy.*

Dae strode forward and held out a hand. "Daniel MacLeod of the clan MacLeod. Lovely to meet you."

Ben closed his eyes in mortification. Oh hell. Dae had gotten his inspiration from watching *Highlander*. He hoped Hemmy hadn't picked up on that little nugget.

Hemmy stood up with a grin and shook Dae's hand. "I thought you were feeling ill, glad to see you feel better. Yeah, Ben here told me you were visiting from Scotland. Great to meet more of this bloke's family at last. I only know his dad. Malcolm is such a hoot. I love the old guy."

Dae blinked, looking intrigued. "Oh, does he live around here too, then?"

Ben nodded quickly. "He stays a village over, I see him fairly often. He's retired now."

Hemmy chuckled. "It took a while for Ben to take me to meet him, though. I was beginning to think my friend here was a changeling found under a bush."

Dae's eyes lit up. "Oh, I doubt that. In my extensive experience, changelings are usually notoriously bad-tempered and rather vicious. Ben here's as soft as a dandelion." He waved a manicured hand, on which various rings resided, one a rather large diamond. "If he were a true changeling, mind, I'd have to do my duty and return him to the realm from whence he came, and that can sometimes be a singularly spectacular event involving exploding parts and a lot of fuss and mess. So it's good he was born from mortals."

Ben laughed anxiously as Hemmy regarded Dae with large eyes and a look of confusion on his face. "Hah, you and your Dungeons and Dragons talk, Dan. So confusing for the rest of us. Do you think you can move out of character and leave the game behind now? In fact," he ushered Dae into the kitchen. "Come help me make coffee."

Once there, he saw Hemmy settle onto the couch, watching them with a degree of puzzlement.

Ben leaned in close to the Djinn. "Behave," he muttered into Dae's ear. "Remember you're a damn human tonight."

Dae scowled. "Fine. He started it, talking of changelings." His eyes narrowed. "You haven't even complimented me on my outfit or my accent. I thought I did rather well."

Ben rolled his eyes. "You look extremely dapper, and while I'm not too sure on the whole Highlander thing, your accent is acceptable. Don't overdo it."

Dae rubbed his chin thoughtfully. "It was either that or some man who thinks he's rather funny called Billy Connolly. I couldn't understand a damned word he said though, so went with Connor instead."

"Thank God for small mercies," Ben murmured. "I don't think I could have dealt with you sounding like Billy." He fiddled with the coffeemaker. "Now go over there and keep Hemmy company, and make sure you stick to normal conversation."

"Fine." Dae flounced back to the lounge and sat down on the other end of the couch. Ben took out three mugs and opened the fridge to get the milk.

"Tell me about yourself," he heard Dae say. "What exactly do you and Ben get up to at the zoo?"

Ben heaved a sigh of relief as Hemmy launched into an enthusiastic account of his job. At least that was a safe subject. He finished making coffee and took it over, setting the three mugs down on the coffee table. Ben got settled in his armchair and smiled over at Hemmy.

"You ready for more episodes of *Mindhunter*? We're starting season two."

Hemmy nodded gleefully. "Oh yeah, bring it on. I can't wait to see what the guys are up to next." He motioned to Dae. "You watched this series before?"

Dae shook his head slowly. "No, I haven't. What's it about?"

"It's about these two FBI guys who go around the US interviewing serial killers so they can gain an insight into what makes them tick and maybe solve some questions at the same time. It's epic."

"Serial killers?" Dae echoed with a moue of distaste. "That's your evening entertainment, watching sick people who kill other people?" His accent slipped a little, but luckily he quickly regained it.

Hemmy looked taken aback and Ben hastened to stop whatever diatribe Dae might be planning. "It's more about the premise behind it, not the violence, Dae—Dan. This was the first unit set up to do this sort of forensic psychology so it could be used going forward to catch killers by seeing patterns in their behaviour. It's really interesting."

Dae took a sip of his coffee. "I see. Well, I'll give it a try." He leaned back against the couch and got comfortable. "Uhm, Ben, did you forget you had something in the oven? It smells done, whatever it is."

Ben shot to his feet. "Shit, I forgot. The Chinese." He scooted over to the oven and opened it as steam billowed out, fogging up the kitchen. With a muttered expletive, he removed the boxes of food, cursing again as he burnt his fingers.

"Right, come and get it. Help yourselves, there's plenty to go around." He opened the cupboard, took out three plates, and set them down. "Knives and forks in the drawer, you know where the stuff is."

Ten minutes later, the three men were once back again in their places, with plates laden with food and tucking into their supper.

The series began and Ben dimmed the lights as the opening credits sounded. Half an hour in, Ben had to suppress a chuckle. Dae was getting into the episode and if the frustrated look on Hemmy's face was anything to go by, the Djinn was about to get an earful about interrupting with questions during the show.

Sometimes life was simple, and with friends like he had, Ben had lucked out.

I could get used to this. Having Dae around permanently.

He sighed softly. That wasn't something he should get behind. Dae was a magical being who'd live forever, and Ben was mortal.

Forget it. Don't start something that has no future.

At least he still had two wishes to change his life.

***

"So, Dan, Ben tells me you're an expert in the energy field. Exactly what is it you do?" The marathon session of *Mindhunter* over—Dae had enjoyed the series but three episodes was enough for him. They'd all settled down with a glass of wine—beer in Hemmy's case—to chat.

Dae was ready for questions. He'd been looking forward to putting his research into play. Ben's sudden twitchiness caused him some amusement though.

This is your fault, gorgeous. Live with it.

Dae waved a hand airily. "Oh, he's too kind. I wouldn't say expert, exactly. I'm a research assistant in the renewable energy field for a company in Edinburgh. I analyse energy storage for the EU, forecasting models and looking at project economics. It's extremely data-driven and challenging, but I love my job."

"Wow." Hemmy's eyes were wide and he carried a look of respect on his face. "That sounds awesome. Ben says you're on a sabbatical. What's all that about?"

Ben stood up. "Another drink anyone?"

Hemmy shook his head. "I'm good."

Ben gathered the glasses and went over to the kitchen to fill up. Dae grinned. *Here I go. You asked for it, Bennie boy.*

"I broke up with my girlfriend and needed some time out to heal my heart." He made a moue of sadness. At the same time, he heard a choking sound from the kitchen and he and Hemmy both looked over curiously to see Ben leaned over the sink, chest heaving.

"You okay, my man?" Hemmy asked solicitously. "What's going on there?"

Ben looked up, his face flushed as he wiped his mouth. "Nothing. Something went down the wrong way." He cast an anxious glance at Dae, who wasn't sure what his frantic gaze was saying. Had he slipped up, and wasn't he supposed to be an energy expert anymore?

Hemmy nodded and turned back to Dae. "Hmm, I don't want to speak out of turn here, but Ben here said you had a boyfriend, a power-builder from Russia? Did I misunderstand something?"

Now it was Dae's turn to choke on his tongue. "A what?" he squeaked, noticing Ben's frantic gestures from the kitchen. "A Russian body-builder boyfriend?"

How the fuck had Ben not told him of this relevant detail? The man was a moron. Dae, though, was a master at a quick recovery in many ways.

"Oh, Sergei? No, I broke up with him some time ago, he was getting too muscly for my tastes. I like 'em leaner. Ben is out of touch with my varied love life."

Hemmy blinked. "Oh, okay, that explains it. Well, I'm sorry to hear about the breakups. That sucks."

"Yes, it does," Dae agreed. "I've made a promise to myself to have no more relationships. I'm going to play fast and loose for a while. Enjoy myself."

Ben came back and leaned in to hand Dae his glass of wine. "Here you go." His gaze held thanks for Dae's quick-wittedness, and he sank into his chair, biting his nails anxiously.

Dae nodded sagely. "I'll be staying here for a little while, hopefully not too long, then I'll be going home. It's all a little up in the air right now."

Hemmy held up his beer bottle. "I hear you. Sometimes these things take time." He drained his beer. "It's getting late, I'd better be off."

He stood up and stretched, his tee-shirt riding up, revealing the soft curve of his belly. "I plan on staying in bed the whole day tomorrow and only getting out of it to have a pee or make me some more coffee. You guys got any plans for the weekend at all?" He shrugged into his now-dry large parka and wrapped the thing closed, then reached into his pocket to pull out a bright red beanie, which he settled onto his curly hair.

Dae looked over at Ben. "I'm not sure. Do we have plans?"

Ben looked a little guilty. "Well, I told Ryan—you know, the son of the guy who owns the antiques place—that I'd accompany him to a gay club in Winchester."

Dae narrowed his eyes. "You have a date?" He wasn't sure he liked that idea. Who was this upstart Ryan anyway in Ben's life?

"Oh God, no," Ben said quickly. "Ryan's too young for me. He's new in the gay club scene so I said I'd go with him, put him at ease."

"Yeah, and the fact he wants into your pants isn't a consideration?" Hemmy guffawed as he wrapped his woolly scarf around his neck, looking as if he was going on an Arctic expedition. "You could tap that, man, and he'd be quite happy."

Tap that? What the hell did that mean? Dae frowned. "Tap what?"

Ben went a bright red. "It's slang. It doesn't matter what it means, it won't be happening."

Hemmy gave another deep bellow of laughter. "You don't know what tapping someone is?" His face crinkled mischievously. "It means bang him, show him the sausage, get into his pants, have sex."

Dae's temper rose. "Really?" he drawled silkily. "Ben, you know you're welcome to bring anyone home when you need to 'tap them.' Don't let me stand in your way." He had no idea why the idea of Ben having sex with anyone else enraged him so. He'd been living with Ben for less than a week. "Put a scarf or something on the door so I know not to barge in the next morning with your coffee. I'd hate to interrupt you mid-coitus."

Ben scowled and cast a fierce glance at a still-amused Hemmy. "Weren't you leaving?" he growled at his friend. "There will be no tapping going on anytime soon, so both of you, let it go." He hustled Hemmy towards the door. "Always a pleasure, Hem," he huffed. "I believe your bed is calling."

Ben opened the door and pushed his friend out into the cold. "Drive safely and see you at work Thursday."

Hemmy waved at them. "Will do. Great meeting you, Daniel. See you soon." He strolled down the garden path and out onto the pavement. They watched him get into his car and drive away, then Ben pulled the door shut. He began picking up all the empty food cartons and glasses while Dae assisted.

"I meant what I said," Dae muttered. "I don't want to be an intrusion. If you ever want to bring a guy home, don't let me stop you." *Even though it will piss the hell out of me, and I might turn the man into a cockroach.* Dae still had enough magic left in him to accomplish that feat, although he preferred not to waste it. It was a limited resource, especially here on earth.

"I told you, I have no intention of bringing anyone home." Ben ran hot water into the sink. "I'm quite happy with things the way they are."

"Hmm." Dae wasn't convinced. He was finding his current state of celibacy a bit of an issue and surely Ben was feeling the same? Back in Calado'r, there'd been so many men for Dae to choose from he'd been spoilt for choice. Truth be told, he'd been rather a man-slut in the lamp, fucking anything he fancied, anything to take his mind off Aether and his betrayal.

Dae picked up a dishcloth with distaste. Wasn't this what dishwashers were made for? It was so plebian to have to physically touch dirty dishes to wash and dry them. He picked up a plate daintily and inspected it for food debris before conceding it was clean and running the dry cloth over it. In Calado'r, he'd never had to worry about things like this.

Yes, the little voice in his head said. *And in Calado'r you didn't have a sexy human man like Ben to share space with. Admit it. You enjoy having him around because he's different to all the sycophants you were used to in the lamp. They were only interested in trying to get free wishes and sleep with a Djinn. They'd suck you off for a promise of riches, fancy new clothes, and luxurious homes. Ben isn't like that.*

"Penny for your thoughts," Ben murmured as he picked up a dishcloth and finished drying the dishes. "You looked as if you were contemplating the woes of the world there for a minute."

Dae huffed. "I was wondering why you don't have a dishwasher. This sort of activity makes my hands terribly dry and does awful things to my nail polish."

Ben snorted. "*That's* what you were thinking about? From the pensive look on your face, I'd have thought you'd figured out how to solve world peace."

Dae blinked. "That's easy. Stop creating wars for stupid reasons of race, territory, religion, sexuality, etc., etc. Accept Mother Earth as the instigator of all things, and the Universe as your world, and prove to her you can protect and love her. That's it. It's not rocket science."

Ben sighed as he hung up his dishcloth. "Would that it could be so easy. I'm not saying I disagree, but that's one colossal culture change for humanity." He switched on the kettle. "Fancy a cup of tea and a shortbread biscuit before bedtime?"

It didn't take Dae long to decide. He did so love the combination of a shortbread biscuit dunked into a hot cup of tea. It had become one of the little pleasures in his current life. "Yes, please."

He'd take his tasty solace to bed with him and tomorrow he'd figure out what to do about these pesky, possessive feelings he had for Ben.

Chapter 8

There was something comforting about cuddling up in bed with a duvet lying over him, enjoying the sound of the birds outside and the steady rhythm of someone breathing next to him. Ben smiled in his sleepy state and snuggled down farther into the warm body behind him—*wait, what the fuck?*

He rolled over, yelping when he saw Dae lying stomach down, eyes closed, his long hair tousled across the pillow. Soft breaths emanated from pink, full lips. For the first time, Ben noticed the shadows beneath the Djinn's eyes and the slight vee between his brows. His bed partner might look at rest, but something wasn't right.

Ben couldn't help himself, he lifted the duvet and saw Dae's naked body was as expected: a sexy heap of curves and planes. One of his long, tanned legs peeked out from beneath, his foot an elegant arch. One hand was scrunched between the pillow and his face, while the other lay over the bed cover. Ben wanted oh so much to move the covers to see the beautiful tattoo on Dae's back again, and take in the splendour that was his Djinn.

Tentatively, he reached out one hand towards Dae to brush a strand of hair away from his face. Then he came to his senses and pulled it back. *He isn't your Djinn, matey, and touching him when he's sleeping is creepy.*

As quietly as he could, Ben shuffled out of bed, glad he was wearing his favourite pair of flannel GI Joe pyjama bottoms. His morning erection tented the material, and the sooner Ben showered and got rid of it the better.

He froze on his way to the bathroom as Dae muttered drowsily, "Aether, is that you? Are you going to let me come home? I've missed you so much."

Who the hell was Ether? Feeling somewhat disgruntled since Dae was in *his* bed, thinking about someone else, Ben slid into the bathroom and locked the door. He stepped out of his pants and started the shower, stepping in and yowling a little as he hadn't left it long enough to get hot.

"Huh," he muttered as he washed his hair and armpits. "Sneaks into my bed at night and ends up dreaming about somebody else. That's enough to dent a man's ego." He worked up a lather and washed his balls and thighs. His dick was still hard, and he decided to give it a helping hand. He closed his eyes, thinking of the sleeping man in his bed and the curve of his delicious arse and back.

He stroked himself slowly, enjoying the build-up of sensation in his groin as he humped into his hand. Back and forward, slick and tight, the way he liked it. If he'd been in bed, he might have pushed a couple of fingers inside himself to make himself come. Here in the shower, though, there was something completely decadent about jerking off when the man invading his thoughts was a few feet outside the door.

His hands fisted his cock harder and harder, and the more Ben thought about Dae filling him up while he lay captured beneath that toned, sexy body, a prisoner at the mercy of the man pumping into him, holding him down, twisting his face to take his mouth in a dirty, open-mouthed kiss…

"Jesus," Ben gasped as he came all over his hands and the shower wall. "Fuck, that was good. Holy shit." He leaned his forehead against the cool tiles, his breath coming in gasps of pleasure. The warm water cascaded over his hair and body, soft touches, which made him shiver with the aftershock of a great orgasm. Once his breathing was under control, Ben turned off the shower and stepped onto the bath mat. His legs still felt a little jellied, and he grinned at his image in the mirror.

"Morning," he said to himself. "Enjoyed that, did you?" He wrapped a towel around his waist, using another to towel dry his hair. He hung it on the towel warmer and opened the door as billows of steam entered the bedroom.

Dae was still there, but he was awake, sitting up in bed with the duvet pooled around his hips. He looked over at Ben and smiled uncertainly.

"Morning."

"Good morning." *Hell, I hope he didn't hear me having a morning wank.*

Ben walked over to the cabinet, which doubled as a dressing table. He picked up his deodorant stick and skimmed it over his pits. He wasn't a fan of aerosols when he could help it. They weren't good for the planet.

"I suppose you're wondering what I'm doing here in your bed?"

Ben had never heard Dae sound so unsure of himself.

He shrugged as he pulled the towel away and dried his body. He was gratified to hear a soft gasp behind him. "You'll tell me when you're ready. I imagine you had a good reason." He finished drying himself and opened the drawer to take out a pair of boxers. Once he was finished pulling them on, he turned around. "Did you sleep well, at least?"

Dae's face darkened. "I had a bit of a bad dream last night. I'm surprised you didn't hear me."

Ben laughed as he pulled on his Windward Zoo polo shirt, then walked over to the hanging closet to retrieve a pair of jeans. "I'm one of those people everyone hates. Someone who can get to sleep within seconds, and sleeps like the dead. There could be a thunderstorm or an earthquake and I probably wouldn't wake up."

Dae leaned back against the pillows, the duvet slipping and revealing an intriguing dip between waist and hip. "I woke up feeling as if I needed some company. I'm sorry if I overstepped any boundaries. I meant to wake up before you and leave, but I guess you beat me to it."

Now dressed, Ben sat down on the bed to pull on his socks and shoes. "I'm not upset, honest. If you needed someone to be there for you, I'm happy to be that person." He stood up. "The birds wake me in the morning. They seem to love performing a full orchestra at seven. They're a natural alarm clock."

He ran some moisturizer over his face and slipped on his smartwatch. "Are you feeling better though? You look a little peaked. Anything I can do to help?"

Dae shook his head. "No, thank you." He laughed bitterly. "Coming to this world appears to have taken away the security blanket I had when I was in Calado'r."

Ben sat down next to him. *Oh God, am I causing him to hurt by not giving him my wishes so he can go home?* No matter how much

Ben wanted to get to know more about Dae, that was something he couldn't justify. It was selfish.

"Am I contributing to the problem?" Ben asked gently. Dae's beautiful purple eyes stared back at him with apprehension. "I mean, do I need to use my wishes so you can return to the lamp and get that security blanket back? I don't want you to feel unhappy here."

Dae smiled faintly and pressed a finger against Ben's lips. "No, Ben. I need to work through this and let go. Coming here allows me to do this. Thanks for the offer."

He stood up, gathering the duvet around his lower half. "You have to get to work. I'd better let you go. I promise not to make a habit of climbing into your bed at night."

Dae shuffled out of the bedroom, closing the door behind him. Ben sighed and got to his feet. He wanted to stay home and be with Dae, but duty called. He was on a later shift today and had another swimming lesson with Sammy. Plus his favourite vet, Alison, was coming by to do an annual health check on the seal and penguin community. Hazel would kill him if he didn't turn up for that. His boss had inventive ways of making people pay for their indiscretions.

No hardship. Ben rather liked Alison. She was a no-nonsense American woman with a wicked sense of humour and a real love for the animals she cared for. Looking after penguins was a complicated affair, and making sure their dietary requirements were met and providing regular check-ups and vitamins was part of her job, as well as Ben's.

He sighed. Best get some breakfast down him and scoot off to work. Perhaps giving Dae some space would let him work out whatever was ailing him.

***

Sweet fucking silver sands. What the holy frinkx was I thinking? Dae dropped Ben's duvet—he'd have to return it and make Ben's bed later—and slumped onto his bed, hands behind his head, scowling at the wall. *I had the perfect opportunity to tell Ben to use his wishes so I can go home, and instead of embracing that eagerly, I went and said that wasn't what I needed.*

"This place is making me crazy," Dae muttered moodily as he fidgeted with the chain around his neck. "I'm infected with humanity and it's making me irrational." He wiggled his toes, watching his blue painted toenails, and huffed.

Remnants of the dream that had driven him into Ben's comforting bed remained in the haziness of his psyche. Fuzzy memories of the brutal punishment he'd received at the request of Lady Brinil, who looked on regally, her sapphire blue eyes glinting with malicious satisfaction at his torment. Her Haughtiness had taken the dalliance of her darling Lord Regent Aether with a nobody from the court personally. It was true that the female of the species was often the deadliest.

"Oh, get over it," Dae muttered to himself as he shuffled out of bed and went over to the window. Outside, a songbird trilled on a leafy branch and a man taking his dog for a walk watched as the animal peed against a tree. "It's been five years." He pulled on his robe and tied the sash. He'd have a shower after Ben left for work.

Covered enough to have breakfast, he left the bedroom and went into the kitchen. Ben sat there, newspaper spread before him as he demolished what looked like marmalade toast. A steaming cup of coffee sat on the kitchen counter by his crumb-speckled plate. He looked up as Dae entered, and Tess gave a woof of greeting.

"You feeling better?" Ben popped a piece of toast into his mouth.

Dae nodded as he poured himself a cup of coffee. "Yes, thank you." He sat down next to Ben and took a sip of his drink. "I'm sorry I surprised you this morning. It won't happen again."

Ben looked puzzled. "I said I didn't mind. If it helps you through your nightmares, I'm okay with it." His face flushed. "It was nice to wake up to someone in bed with me. That hasn't happened in a while."

Dae frowned. "Why ever not? You're a handsome man. I'd have thought you'd have your choice of suitors."

Ben laughed. "You think? This is a small village, not a lot of men here with the same tastes as me. At least, none who will admit to it. While I enjoy the club scene, I'm not much into one-night stands."

Dae narrowed his eyes. "You have Ryan, who from all accounts sounds as if he'd be happy to be your bed buddy." *And doesn't that thought sting?*

Ben's eyes widened. "Oh hell no. As I said, he's young and starting out. I'm not what he needs. Anyway, he's not my type."

That was a great segue into finding out where Ben's taste in men lie, and Dae jumped on it. "What is your type then?" Dae murmured silkily.

Ben cleared his throat and fiddled with a small piece of toast. Tess, sitting at his side, looked at it longingly. He sighed and held the piece down to her, and she took it gently. "Well, most guys I've been with have been like—" he hesitated, "well, like you."

"Interesting," Dae mused as he rubbed his chin. "You like them slim and sassy? With tons of sex appeal, a quicksilver mind, and sharp wits?"

Ben smiled, a wide one that lit up his face, and Dae nearly swooned. "You do have a high opinion of yourself, don't you? But yes, I guess."

Dae shifted on the chair, artfully letting his robe slid off his leg to reveal his tanned thigh. He didn't miss Ben's hitch of breath. *Score one for the Djinn.*

Dae reached over and trailed his fingers along Ben's hand, speckled with hair, strong and calloused. He was a man who worked with his hands, and Dae loved their strength and roughness. Ben swallowed and cleared his throat. His eyes darkened as he watched Dae's fingers strum their song on his hand. Dae turned it over and stared down at his palm as he grinned to himself.

"Hmm, you have a long lifeline—go you—but this love line looks a little…neglected. It tells me you're rather depleted in the sex department. You prefer a relationship to a casual fuck, and you've still to find the man who satisfies you. I also see a man, close to you, who desires you and wants to fulfil *your* desires." He traced the faint love line on Ben's palm gently. "You deserve to have a special someone in your life to keep you sated."

He looked up at Ben's wide-eyed gaze and congratulated himself on being so wily.

"Wow, you can see all of that in my palm? I'm impressed. I mean, who knew?" Ben withdrew his hand and reached for his mobile. He dialled a number.

"What are you doing?" Dae asked in confusion.

"Calling Ryan to make sure we're on for Friday. I mean, if I'm *meant* to be with him, then I suppose I should do a little wooing before I get laid on Friday." The phone rang on the other side.

"What the fuck?" Dae sputtered. "That's not what I meant at all. Terminate that call immediately." He reached for the mobile, but Ben held it away, chuckling.

"You can't tell me to go for my dream then take it away from me. What kind of genie are you?"

"Djinn," Dae fumed. "Now hang up. I wasn't talking about Ryan, that little shoodlepopper."

"Oh?" Ben raised one brow in amusement. "Then who were you referring to?" He sniggered. "And what the hell is a shoodlepopper?"

Dae finally grabbed the phone and held it to his ear in triumph. "Hah, if that upstart answers, I'll—"

He was interrupted by a broad East London accent. "Hey, Ben, what's up? You calling me for a booty call?"

Dae stared at the phone in horror as he saw Ben in splutters of laughter, bent over in mirth. "A booty call? Who the hell is this?"

Ben recovered enough to snatch the phone away and answer. "Hi, Darrall. Sorry, I must've pocket dialled you. Don't mind my friend. He was trying to be clever, but it backfired." He continued to have a conversation while Dae looked on in frustration. Finally Ben winked at him. "Cheers, mate. Nice to catch up. I'll see you soon, yeah?" He rang off and laid his phone down, still chuckling.

Dae glared at him. "You son of a banshee, you set me up," he said frostily. "You were never calling Ryan."

Ben shrugged his shaking shoulders. "Sorry, but you were so into it, and I knew you were bullshitting me." His chuckles subsided. A speculative expression crossed his face. "I'd love to know, though, who you were referring to in your Madam Zara impression. Was it perhaps you?" He stood up and moved over to Dae, whose mouth had suddenly gone dry. He uttered a squeak as Ben reached out and caressed his jawline. *Oh God, his fingers are as rough as I thought they'd be, and they feel incredible on my skin.* His back grew warm as his tattoo came to life with the seductive touches.

"Am I allowed to accept your invitation? We've been living together for nearly a week and I think we both want whatever this is building between us." Ben's thumb ran along Dae's bottom lip, his touch filled with a promise of more to come.

Dae hadn't counted on Ben making the first move. The man standing before him, with a flash of heat in his eyes and his voice husky with want, was a world away from the often grumpy yet sexy individual he'd grown used to.

"Do you know I jerked off in the shower this morning thinking about you? You were lying in my bed and I so wanted to move the covers away and see that gorgeous tattoo up close and personal."

Underneath his flimsy gown, Dae's cock swelled and brushed against the silk, making him groan in pleasure. On his back, skin fluttered and tickled as his tattoo responded to the caresses.

"You did? Why didn't you call me to shower with you?" Dae's nerve endings were on fire, synapses firing with pinpricks of welcomed heat.

Ben leaned in and nuzzled Dae's neck. "I didn't know if it was what you wanted. I'm not a man who presumes." His lips brushed against Dae's warm skin.

Dae closed his eyes at the soft kisses being planted down his throat. "I find you so damned sexy, how could you not know that? You're amazi—" His words were swallowed as Ben's lips took his, demanding and rough, nothing sweet or soft about it. This was a kiss of sheer want, of animal attraction, and Dae sunk into it like falling into an abyss—scared, exhilarated, dizzy, and breathless. Ben's lips were chapped, tasted of coffee and oranges, and his hands at the back of Dae's neck were demanding, yet soothing, holding Dae in place while his mouth was ravished.

Dae moaned in the back of his throat and stood up, pressing himself against Ben's body. The hardness of Ben's length pressed into his stomach and Dae wanted nothing more than to get down on his knees and worship the cock that was straining to be released. He licked at the inside of Ben's mouth one last time then slid down onto the floor.

Ben's mouth was swollen, his face dazed and he groaned. "Jesus, Dae, please. Need to feel your mouth around me."

"Oh, don't worry," Dae promised as he expertly unzipped Ben and rubbed the heel of his hand over the cock within, the front of Ben's briefs already wet with desire. "I'll give you what we both want."

Ben's cock sprung free and Dae pushed the jeans farther down so he could get a grip on the base. Ben gave another loud groan and pushed forward. Dae wasted no time. He slid his lips over the tip and flicked his tongue. Ben's hips stuttered forward and he grunted apologetically when he lightly grasped Dae's head. "Sorry, can't help it. Tell me if it's too much."

Dae didn't bother replying since his mouth was full of salty, uncut cock and he was treating it as he would a delicious ice cream. Mouth going round and round, up and down, suck and release with the occasional pressure of tongue on Ben's sensitive and intimate places. Dae kept the pressure on with his hand, delaying Ben's gratification. His free hand was wrapped around his cock and he fisted it fiercely.

This wasn't the time for slow and tender. This was primal, and all Dae wanted was to make them both come—make both of them smell of come and sweat, and be spent and dishevelled in the privacy of the kitchen.

Bedroom action could come later, and Dae knew full well how he wanted that to happen. He wanted to slide his cock inside Ben, touch him inside and out, control him, watch his face as Dae thrust back and forwards, and touched Ben's heart with his dick.

The thought of it sped up Dae's hand on his swollen member and he was close to coming. From the soft pants and moans coming from Ben, he thought he might be too.

Dae tightened his aching jaw around Ben and sucked as if his life depended on it.

"Oh Jesus," Ben panted. "So good, don't stop." His hands pressed more firmly into Dae's skull, and he loved it.

Loved when a man directed him and made him feel powerful, knowing he could drive him crazy with lust. Ben shouted out something intelligible, and Dae's mouth filled with spunk. He drew back, swallowing the musky-scented gift, and then as Ben collapsed panting against the island, Dae licked at the residue, leaning Ben up best he could.

Still on his knees, he tugged forcefully at himself, the pins and needles in his skin increasing as his balls drew up and he climaxed with a gasp. His seed painted the bottom of

Ben's legs and spilled onto his tangled jeans, as well as all over Dae.

"Oops," Dae said huskily. "It's a bit of a mess down here. You may need another shower and a change of clothes before you go to work."

Ben chuckled and reached out a hand to tug Dae to his feet. "That's okay. I'm due in at twelve. Perhaps we can take that shower together?"

Dae smiled as he stood up and gave Ben a lingering kiss. "That could work out well. Any excuse for me to touch you again. I'm an expert at soaping up."

Ben grinned and took Dae's hand. "If this is my life, I'm on board with it. Not every man can say he's had his cock sucked by a genie." He tugged Dae along to the bathroom.

Dae followed willingly. He wasn't sure where this would end up, but for now, he was right where he wanted to be.

Chapter 9

"*This* is your idea of a bar?" Dae's nose wrinkled in distaste as he stood shivering in the queue to get into *Do Cum In*. "One has to stand in line like a commoner and subject oneself to being prodded and poked by passers-by?" He shot a dangerous glare at the man who jostled him from behind. "If you touch my arse one more time, I will turn you into a fucking lizard. Back off."

The man laughed. "He's a feisty one," he said to Ben admiringly. "Perhaps I'll look you both up on the dance floor."

Ben bit back a chuckle. He'd like to see the guy try given the look Dae was currently sporting. He moved a little behind the Djinn, more to try to protect the stranger than out of any sense of decorum to protect Dae's sensibilities. He was sure his friend could look after himself. Of course, Dae looking like a delicious morsel of sheer sexy in his black see-through silk blouse and tight white trousers, wearing that chain of his that reached from wrist to bicep, wasn't going to stop unwanted attention.

"Could you honestly turn him into a lizard?" Ben murmured into Dae's ear. "Do you have that kind of magic here on earth?"

Dae huffed. "My magic is less here, but yes, I could. It isn't generally advisable to do so, though. It drains me, gives me a bit of a headache." He pushed a piece of hair back from his eyes. "I would gladly suffer it if that muckdweller keeps ghosting my backside."

Ben snorted. "You have a unique vocabulary of insults. I need to keep a notepad nearby so I can write them down."

"Hey, guys." Ben turned as Ryan walked up to them, cheeks ruddy and a hesitant smile on his face. "I made it. Sorry I'm late." He cast an appreciative look at Dae. "Wow, Ben, hooked up already? You lucky bastard, you."

"You must be Ryan," Dae said frostily. "Ben hasn't 'hooked up' as you so delightfully put it. We came together."

"I bet you did," Ryan joked and squawked as Dae poked him fiercely with a finger tipped with black nail polish.

"Not funny. Did Ben not explain I was his roommate, and his cousin?"

Ben thought it was time to stop the amusing interchange and grinned as he moved in between the two men.

"Guys, settle down. Dan, this is Ryan, my friend from the antiques shop. Ryan, this is Dan. He's my cousin from Scotland who's visiting...." His voice trailed off as he realised Dae had spoken normally and not in his faux Scottish accent. Shit. He'd have to make sure that Hemmy and Ryan weren't together when Dae was around, or the cat would be out of the bag.

"You don't *sound* Scottish," Ryan said doubtfully, brow furrowed.

Dae sniffed and cast a wary look at Ben, obviously remembering who he was supposed to be. "I only live there. I'm not a native Scot."

"Oh. Well, nice to meet you, Dan. If you're not with Ben..." Ryan cast a speculative look at Dae's outfit. "Maybe we can get together inside for a dance...or more?" He smirked and Ben rolled his eyes.

Over my dead body are you getting frisky with my *Djinn.*

"Listen, Ryan, I said I'd come with you tonight to be backup. I didn't ask you to hit on my cousin, all right? Find your own man to get down and personal with."

Ryan frowned. "Have to say I don't get the family resemblance. Are you sure you two are related?"

Ben was saved the trouble of answering as the doors open and the crowd surged forward. As they shuffled closer to the entrance, Dae leaned in to whisper in Ben's ear.

"My, we are possessive, aren't we? You do realise we can't get up to any hanky-panky inside as I'm family? You didn't think this one through."

Ben hadn't thought of that and his heart sank. Any grinding up and getting sexy on the dance floor would have to wait for the privacy of home. Damn.

Since the epic blowjob they'd shared a couple of days ago, and a sensuous post-sex shower massage, he and Dae hadn't gone any further. Sure, there'd been a few stolen kisses here and there, but no more.

Dae gave a sexy chuckle. "I can see that realisation coming to roost. No matter. I'm sure there's plenty more talent for us to enjoy inside. It looks like Ryan is already getting his groove on." He waved a hand behind them. Ben turned to see that Ryan was in animated conversation with some other young twenty-something, and the two of them appeared to be getting along, as evidenced by their sly touches.

The nightclub was buzzing as they finally paid their entrance fee—much to Dae's disgust—and stepped inside. Despite Ryan having said he wanted company to assist him on his first jaunt into a gay club, he wasted no time disappearing to the bar with the guy he'd met outside. He waved at Ben and Dae apologetically as he disappeared into the throng.

Ben motioned over to an open table. "Looks like he doesn't need any moral support. Let's grab that space, and then I'll get us a drink." He had to shout a little over the raucous strains of dance music. Dae nodded and followed Ben over to a table along the wall. They'd been lucky—most of them were already filled.

"What do you want to drink?" Ben asked. He was ready for a beer.

"Grab me a double gin and tonic," Dae replied as he surveyed the room with appreciative eyes. "I'll start off easy."

Ben fought his way through the grinding couples on the dance floor to get to the bar. Ryan was in among the dancers, beer in hand as he shimmied with the stranger he'd met. He saw Ben and lifted his bottle in a wave.

It was a bit of a wait, but eventually Ben had their drinks and he made his way back to the table. He was irked to see someone perched in his chair, already seemingly staking a claim on his— what, boyfriend? Friend? Exactly what was Dae to him other than a friend with benefits? That knowledge irritated Ben and when he reached the table, he put the drinks down with more force than was necessary.

Dae looked up at him with a grin. "I thought you'd gotten lost. Rory here was telling me about this amazing place he explored in Puerto Rico. He's an archaeologist and has a fascinating job."

Ben regarded the other man—a thirty-something ginger-haired, brawny man with an impressive set of muscles—and tried to smile politely. "That does sound interesting." Rory didn't offer to give up his seat so Ben stood there awkwardly, not wanting to cause a scene demanding his chair back.

"Nice to meet you," Rory said. "Your cousin here is quite something, isn't he?" He stared at Dae, lust flickering in his eyes. Ben wanted to poke them out with a fire stick. No one should look at Dae that way other than him.

He had a sudden pleasurable thought. He could use one of his wishes to transport this unwanted intruder to a faraway place — perhaps Puerto Rico, since he seemed to love it so much.

Dae's finger circled the rim of his glass seductively and Ben wanted to growl as Rory's fascination found another focus.

"My cousin is indeed special," Ben grunted. "I bet he could make all your dreams come true. Do you fancy another trip to Puerto Rico then?" He rubbed his chin. "Now let me see, how does it go?" He pursed his lips. "I think it starts, 'Oh Djinn of the lamp'—"

Dae's eyes widened in apprehension. "Whoa, Ben. What the hell do you think you're doing?"

Rory was staring at them, his face creased in a smile. "You two are a bit weird, aren't you? Why would I want to go to Puerto Rico when everything I want is here in this sexy little package?" He leered at Dae and that was it. Ben was not only ready to vomit, but he was also ready to fulfil one of his wishes. "Oh Djinn—"

He was stopped by Dae rising hastily and pressing a firm finger to his lips. "Benjamin Arthur Sinclair, don't you dare complete that sentence. You should be ashamed of yourself." He turned to a stupefied Rory. "I'm sorry, love, but it appears he's lost his mind. Would you be a sweetheart and go get me another gin and tonic from the bar while I have a quiet word with him?" Dae gave the man a sweet smile and Rory melted.

"Sure, sexy. I can do that. Don't go anywhere, 'kay?" With one last adoring look, Rory disappeared into the throng. As soon as he was gone, Dae turned to Ben.

"What the sweet silver sands do you think you were doing? Are you honestly willing to waste one of your wishes on something as stupid as wishing poor Rory away?"

"He's annoying me," Ben said between gritted teeth. "The man doesn't understand the concept of personal space."

"Oh, my dear, sweet, stupid man." Dae looked at him pityingly. "You have been in a gay bar before, right? That concept doesn't exist here. I'm beginning to worry which one of you is the novice." He motioned to Ryan grinding against yet another man on the dance floor. "That young man has more of the concept of what to do here than you do."

"There's plenty of others here your beau can focus on," Ben shot back. "You were encouraging him."

Dae's gaze grew speculative with a soupçon of satisfaction. "Son of a banshee, you're jealous." His smile widened. "I didn't expect this side of you. It's sexy."

Ben slumped down into the seat Rory vacated. He wouldn't be getting it back, he thought in victory. "I'm not jealous." *I fucking am. How can I argue that?* "It's rude to hit on another man's guy when that man's guy is right here, in his face…" His voice trailed off. Shit, this was becoming complicated. They didn't have a relationship. All Dae was having was a bit of fun before he granted Ben's wishes and went back to his magical life in the lamp. This was no long-term thing. How could it be?

Dae sighed and sat back down. He reached over and took Ben's hand in his. "Listen, I know this is strange. Neither of us anticipated the physical attraction between us."

Ben stared at him. "Only physical?" *I don't think it's purely that. I like having you around more than I should.*

Dae's face shadowed. "Well, we both know it can only be that, yes? Anything else would be crazy. After all, we literally come from different worlds. We can't get emotionally attached."

Ben's throat closed up and his stomach clenched. It might be the truth, but did it have to sting so much?

"Yeah, you're right," he grunted. "I think I overreacted. I have no right to claim anything about you. Thanks for putting it into perspective." He stood up. "I'm going to get another drink. Give Rory his seat back. I'll be at the bar if you need me."

Without waiting for Dae's response, he strode into the crowd.

Bollocks. He'd have another drink, get a little rat-faced, then find someone to dance with. Perhaps that would lift his bad mood a little.

***

By Beza's Beard, he hadn't handled that well, had he? With a heavy heart, Dae watched Ben fight his way through the crowd. The man's slumped shoulders made him feel worse.

We can't get attached, no matter how we feel. It simply won't work. Is it wrong to admit the truth?

Dae loved his time with Ben more than he should, but he was under no illusion it could last. Ben would make his two wishes, and then Dae would have no choice but to go back to his world. Why did life have to be so damned complicated?

Rory appeared bearing two glasses, and plonked himself down in the seat Ben had recently vacated. "Here you go, mate. A G and T, and a beer for me." He took a long slurp of his beer then put the glass down with a satisfied belch. "That's better." He looked around. "Your, er, cousin, gone then? You managed to sort him out?"

Dae sighed. "He went to the bar. He won't be back too soon. You're safe." The thing was, as much as Dae appreciated Rory's attention—clearly Dae *was* something of an attention whore—the only man he wanted sitting opposite him was Ben.

"Fancy a dance?" Rory gestured towards the gyrating people behind him. Dae shook his head.

"I'm okay right now. Maybe later. Please, don't let me keep you from it. I see a rather lovely young thing giving you the eye from over there. Perhaps he'll grant you a dance or two." Rory looked over to see what Dae saw, a handsome young man dressed stylishly in chinos and a tight tee giving him a come-hither look while mouthing the words "I love gingers."

Rory glanced back at him. "Sure. I wouldn't want to disappoint anyone. There's plenty of me to go around." He stood and winked at Dae. "Hope I'll see you later then. Enjoy your drink."

Once again, Dae was left alone. He drained his drink, then stood to stretch his legs and see if he could find Ben. He thought he spotted him in the middle of the crowd, but it wasn't light enough to be sure. The only way he'd make sure was to make his way over.

When he got there, he thought he knew how Ben had felt when he'd seen Rory coming onto Dae. Ben was sandwiched between two men, hips gyrating to the music—sweet son of a sea cook, how did the man manage to move like that? It was downright filthy and gave Dae a warm sensation in his groin.

Ben's face shone with sweat and his eyes glinted in laughter as he teasingly swivelled his hips and waved his fingers in a *come and get it* gesture to the short Latinx hottie dancing with him. The other man, lean, with dark red hair and dressed in precious little, had his hands on Ben's waist, under his shirt and was slowly slipping lower.

Oh no, bullshit to that. This wouldn't do. At all. Magic headache be damned, Dae wasn't having these two perverts macking on his friend.

He edged closer to the trio and flexed his fingers. It would only take a teensy bit of effort and he'd make these men pay for treating Ben like a piece of meat. He closed his eyes, thinking of his homeland, Quimaria, and its scented gardens and evergreen hills. As the images conjured in his mind, Dae felt the tingling in his arms that heralded the approach of his magic. He smirked as the pins and needles reached his fingers. Then, with a gesture so subtle he doubted anyone would notice it, he sent a burst of energy straight down into the red-haired man's groin.

The shriek that burst forth from Red's mouth would have shattered glass. Dae winced. He hadn't meant to do *too* much damage—he may have misjudged the amount of magic he used.

He'd been on the receiving end of a *dunzu* spell before, and he knew the feeling of heat and prickling when it hit. It wasn't pleasant, but wouldn't damage anything vital. It was a bit like getting menthol cream on your private bits.

"My fucking balls are on fire," Red screamed as he staggered about, reaching into his tight trousers to relieve himself. "My dick is burning."

Ben stepped away, staring at the unfortunate man's nether regions in horror. "What the hell happened?"

Dae edged closer to Ben, deciding he'd done enough damage for one night. Mr Latinx had already made a wise move and disappeared into the crowd standing around gaping at the man cradling his groin.

"Let me help you," Dae offered. He snatched a glass of beer from a gaping patron. With one quick flick, he threw the contents of the glass over Red's groin.

"There, that should help. Do you need any more? I'm sure one of these lovely people would delight in putting out the fire. You with the drink. Help the poor man."

As various patrons began dousing Red with their drinks, Dae moved over to Ben and grinned. "You seem to attract excitement wherever you go. Perhaps you should have a break from dancing. Come, I'll buy you a drink." He took Ben's hand and dragged him towards the bar. The path was fairly clear as most people were assisting in putting out Red's fire.

Ben looked shocked. "I don't know what the hell happened. One minute we were dancing, the next he was prancing about like a loon. That poor guy. Do you think he'll be okay?" He looked back uncertainly, biting his lip in a way Dae found rather appealing. "Should we call nine-nine-nine or something, get them to take him to the hospital?"

Dae waved a hand airily. "Oh, no need for that. I'm sure whatever is ailing him will clear soon." In his experience, the effects of the *dunzu* receded after about five minutes. However, the effects of casting that bit of magic outside of his kingdom were starting to hit him. Dae's head spun and he had a distinct ache in his bones. He needed water and a bit of fresh air, and he'd be fine.

They reached the bar and Dae ordered another beer and a glass of water.

Ben blinked at him. "You're drinking water? Are you feeling all right?"

Dae was too busy draining the glass to answer. He finished it then slid across the counter to the bartender. "Another one of those, please." He nodded at Ben. "I'm good. Had enough alcohol. Perhaps we can take a walk outside onto the deck when I'm done with this one?" He swigged down his second water as quickly as the first. His head was swimming and his insides felt a little swirly. Drat it. He simply wasn't used to being drained like this anymore.

There'd been a time he could've done magic all day, and only needed to rest at night. Earth was sucking away at his mystical energy like a creature intent on siphoning every last drop of his essence. For one fleeting moment, he wondered why that would be so. His last visits here hadn't affected his magic this way. What had changed?

He didn't have much time to ponder because the lights began to spin around him and his vision grew blurry. He was aware of Ben's concerned expression, and his strong arms wrapping around him as he lost his balance and tumbled to the floor.

Chapter 10

Ben caught Dae as he fell. He'd seen the sudden wooziness cross Dae's face and instinctively reached out to steady him. He hadn't quite expected to find a hundred and eighty pounds of warm, pliable man in his arms.

"I'm fine," Dae gasped as he clutched at Ben's waist. "It's only a silly dizzy spell. Take me outside, please. I need air."

Ben wasted no time in hauling Dae across the dance floor, pushing people out of the way in his haste to get to the deck. He pushed the half-ajar door fully open with his foot and stepped out as Dae took a gasping breath.

"Bouncing Balls, that's better." The Djinn took in a few more deep breaths, his exhales misting before him. Ben held him close, making sure he didn't fall again. At least, that's what Ben told himself.

The scent of Dae's spicy perfume—not aftershave, because the man never seemed to grow hair on his face—brushed his nostrils like the delicate touch of a spring breeze. It was intoxicating and Ben closed his eyes and drank it in.

"Thanks," Dae said quietly, still ensconced in Ben's arms. "I was feeling a little out of it." He leaned back against Ben, his hair tickling Ben's nose. The side of Dae's neck was only centimetres away from Ben's lips and he had the insane desire to kiss it and never stop until he'd reached the dark tattoo peeking out of the top of Dae's shirt. Ben yearned to see it and trace it with his tongue.

"That's okay. Glad I have my uses." Someone was smoking, and the scent of it overlaid Dae's more pleasant fragrance. Ben wrinkled his nose in annoyance. "Couldn't have you face planting in there and hurting yourself."

They stood together in easy silence as their breath frosted and Ben felt the soft throb of Dae's heart against his chest.

"Can I ask you a question?" he asked. "And will you answer me honestly?"

Dae snorted softly. "You can ask, but I can't promise any reply, let alone an honest one."

"How did you come to be in the lamp?" Ben asked quietly. Dae's body stiffened slightly in Ben's arms, and he held him tighter. "Don't go. I promise to accept whatever answer you give me, but I care about you and I'd like to know."

"It's only been six days, Benjamin," Dae muttered but didn't attempt to escape Ben's grasp. "It's a bit of a reach to say you care about me, surely?"

"You don't get to decide how I feel," Ben whispered against Dae's perfect shell ear. He smiled at the shiver that ran through Dae's body. "Your choice is to give me an answer or not. Which one will it be?"

"Given I seem to be your prisoner, I suppose I have no option," Dae said waspishly. Ben grinned. There was his sassy genie. "Fine, I'll give you the details but I need a drink in my hand first. Can we go home, and sit comfortably? Then we can talk."

Ben had no problem with that. "I'll check on Ryan, see if he's okay, then we can get going. Meet me outside by the exit." Reluctantly Ben released his grip on Dae and with a pang of regret, they separated.

"Fine. I'll see you there. Tell Ryan I said good-bye, and I hope he's having fun." Dae brushed past Ben and disappeared inside.

It took a while, but eventually Ben found Ryan hunkered down in a quiet side booth, a smile of pleasure on his face as he huddled close to a man with broad shoulders and a messy shock of chestnut hair. Ryan waved when he saw Ben.

"Hey, Ben, how you doing? Where's Dan?"

Ben motioned behind him. "He's on his way out. We're going home. Everything okay with you?" He nodded at the stranger, who nodded back with a grin. Ryan waved a hand at his tablemate.

"This is Frankie. He's into building restoration, like museums and churches and stuff. Isn't that fascinating? He's been advising on some renovations at Winchester Cathedral, isn't that cool?"

Ben agreed that was indeed cool, and was glad to see Ryan was comfortable in the club.

With a proper good-bye, he made his way to the exit.

***

Tess was pleased at their return and followed Ben everywhere, her tail wagging. He reached down and ruffled her fur. "Good girl. Do you fancy a quick snack while I make some tea?" He looked around guiltily. Dae thought Tess was getting a bit tubby, given Ben's habit of feeding her snacks and—to Dae's horror—pizza slices. Dae was still in the bathroom, brushing his teeth, so Ben slipped Tess a small piece of cold meat from the fridge.

He busied himself making their hot drinks then took the steaming cups through to the lounge. As Ben sat in his chair, Dae wandered through, dressed in his lounging pants and a loose long-sleeved top. He looked vulnerable, not like the sassy smart-mouth Ben was used to.

While Ben wanted to hear Dae's story, the one thing he didn't want was to cause the man undue stress or trauma, especially since he already had nightmares. "If you don't want to talk, that's all right," he murmured, taking a sip of his tea. It was white and sugary, the way he liked it. "I've no claim on you or your story."

Dae unrolled his long limbs gracefully onto the couch, pulling his shirt over his knees and then clasping his arms around them. He stared down at his hands, his hair obscuring his face. "I know that. You aren't forcing me to do anything. I choose to tell you what I'm going to say." He looked up. His beautiful purple eyes looked haunted. Ben noticed faint shadows beneath them. "You'd think I'd be over it all by now, but some things stick and won't go away no matter how much I wish they would."

He took a deep breath. "You need to understand my homeland, Quimaria, is a place of contrast. Our rulers are a mix of empathy and empirical arrogance. Lord Regent Dhimrin— whom you'd call a king here, I suppose, but we called him Lord—was tough, and ruled with an iron hand, but was open to change and progress. Lady Brinil, however," he uttered a harsh laugh, "was not as understanding." He stopped, staring down in contemplation at his feet. Ben waited patiently.

After a while, Dae carried on. "Their son, Master Regent Aether, was the joy of their lives. He was a year younger than me, and the people's hero. Handsome, caring, and always ready to defend the underdog." His lips twisted. "Except when it came to me. The man he should have protected with all his heart."

"You loved him," Ben said, wondering why there was a pang in his chest as he said it. "Did he love you?"

Dae's lips thinned. "I thought so. We met at a lakeside festival when I was with my father. He had a stall selling leather goods and was one of the Lord Regent's favourite leather smiths. Aether took a fancy to a leather bracelet and stopped to convince the Lord to purchase it." Dae smiled at his memory. "I'd been aware of him for many years. He was my greatest fantasy. We got to chatting and arranged a meeting that evening by the lake. I was confused. Why would a Master Regent and heir to the Kingdom want to involve himself with someone like me?" Dae paused. "I went anyway, and it soon became clear he wanted to be more than friends. I didn't resist, and soon meetings by the lake became a way of life for us."

"You became lovers." Ben placed his empty teacup on the side table, fascinated by the story. "Was it not permitted?"

Dae shrugged. "Same-sex relationships are the norm where I'm from. We're pansexual, and choose the person, not the gender. That wasn't the issue. The problem was that Aether had chosen a local boy beneath his station to dally with. He had to hide me from his parents." He grimaced as he cradled his cup in his hands. "His mother, Lady Brinil, suspected something was up and had Aether followed. It wasn't long before I was marched from my home under Regent Guard and taken to Ishvar, the Regent's dwelling. I suppose humans would call it a palace."

"What happened to you?" Ben asked. "Were they the ones who banished you to the lamp?"

Dae snorted, his face hard. "Yes, after they'd beaten me senseless. Any hope I had of redemption or rescue was cruelly quashed with every flick of the whip, every beat of the ivory cane, and every punch of a metalled fist. Aether let it happen." He swallowed and Ben reached out and placed a comforting hand on his shoulder.

Dae reached up and laid his hand over Ben's as if seeking comfort. "My beautiful Aether stood by with his red-rimmed, tearful eyes, watching me being beaten and tormented into admitting I'd seduced and entranced the heir to the kingdom by nefarious means."

"He was scared," Ben said quietly. "Afraid of his parents. Why else would he do that if he professed to love you?"

Dae blew out a breath. "I suppose in hindsight that's probably true." His tone turned bitter. "But when you're lying bleeding in a puddle of your fluids on the floor, it's not easy to accept. His mother had insisted on the punishment. Lord Dhimrin had not been as disposed towards it, but she insisted."

He swallowed. "I refused to give them the satisfaction of admitting to any wrongdoing, much to my families' dismay. Then Lady Brinil came up with the plan to imprison me for life in Calado'r—in the lamp."

Ben gasped in horror. "For the crime of loving someone? That's inhuman."

Dae nodded. "It was only the entreaties of my father, Madeaus, that stopped my eternal descent. As I said, he was a favourite of Lord Dhimrin. Strangely, Lady Mage Elicia was on my side and convinced them to reduce it to ten years with a promise never to see Aether again."

He sighed. "The Lady Mage is Lord Dhimrin's sister, and he holds her in high regard. She was strangely supportive of my predicament and I was lucky and grateful to have in her such a powerful ally." His eyes closed, his face drawn. "It was the pain of knowing Aether did nothing to help me, especially after all our passionate protestations of love, that hurt the most. The physical pain I could deal with." He sighed. "I miss my family, especially my sister. We were always close. I haven't seen them in five of our years, and I won't get to see them for another five until my sentence is served."

There was silence while Ben digested the story and Dae no doubt reflected on the painful memories of his past. Finally, Ben stood and motioned to Dae to scoot over so he could sit next to him. Tenderly, he cupped Dae's cheeks in his hands. Dae's sad gaze cut Ben to the core.

"What happened to you was terrible," Ben muttered. "Those bastards treated you abominably. You didn't deserve any of it. I'm not happy to learn you were taken from your family and your home. There might not be any happy ending to this story, but I'm glad you appeared in my life. I only hope that for the short time you're here, you can enjoy yourself. I promise I'll do my best to get you home—well, to Calado'r—as soon as I can. If that's what you want."

Dae's gaze softened, and he gave a slight nod. "Thank you. I appreciate your kindness. I won't be chasing you for your wishes. I'm quite enjoying it here." He paused. "With you."

Ben lost his breath, but before he could find it, Dae's lips on his stole any semblance of rational thought. The kiss was tender to begin with, but soon evolved into something more urgent with the slick pressure of tongue. Ben's hands slid beneath Dae's shirt, finding warm, fragranced skin.

"Is this okay?" he murmured against Dae's lips.

Dae chuckled sultrily as he gripped Ben's tee-shirt, pulling it over Ben's head. "This is meant to happen, Ben. You're making one of *my* wishes come true."

***

Ben had no idea how they came to be naked in Dae's plush, satin-lined bed—perhaps Dae cast a damn spell on him—and Dae was sprawled across his body feasting on one of his nipples. Dae's tongue lapped at the sensitive nub and Ben's dick was loving the action.

"Holy shit," Ben gasped as Dae bit lightly into his pecs and then trailed his tongue across to Ben's armpit. "I don't even remember how we got to this stage."

Dae looked up, his wicked gaze focusing on Ben, his purple eyes smoky. "You don't remember begging me to take you to bed so we could fuck?"

Ben's dick jumped at the thought. He hazily remembered saying something like that while Dae turned his insides to jelly with lazy strokes to Ben's cock. "Maybe. I, erm, I need to tell you something though before we go any further. I'm not into, you know…" Ben wasn't sure how to address the topic without being too blunt. "Bottoming or topping. Is that a problem?"

He watched Dae pause his exploration of Ben's navel and look up. "*Azizam*, there are plenty of ways to be intimate without being inside one another. I'm glad you told me, though." He winked. "We can get…creative."

Dae climbed up Ben and straddled him across his groin. He leaned forward, and bestowed a soft kiss on him, rocking above him as he did so. Ben gasped as Dae's cock brushed his, harder then harder still until the two of them were moaning loudly.

"See?" Dae said, in between his sexy panting. He smiled wickedly and kept up his momentum. "This feels good too. I love the feeling of your cock on mine." He groaned louder and buried his face in Ben's chest. "Oh God, you are so fucking sexy. You're going to make me come so damned hard." He gave one last gasp, then shuddered and Ben's groin and belly grew wet and warm.

The pleasure of Dae's orgasm and the low moans coming from his flushed throat triggered Ben's climax and soon he too was spilling all over himself and his lover. He gripped Dae's firm cheeks as his body surrendered to the pleasure.

Dae chuckled hoarsely and lifted himself off Ben to roll over and lie on his back. His lithe body relaxed and he lay sprawled in a delightful show of decadence. There was nothing Ben wanted more to see than the beautiful naked front of Dae's body.

He waited for his breathing to return to normal, then rolled onto his side and trailed his fingers across the mess on Dae's stomach. Then he sucked their combined spend off his fingers.

Dae's eyes widened in appreciation. "Frinx, that's sexy, you tasting my come like that."

Ben chuckled. "You make it easy, looking like you do. I have a favour to ask. Will you turn over onto your stomach for me?"

Dae grinned and rolled over lazily. "Should I be jealous of my tattoo? You seem to be more obsessed with it than you are with me."

Ben gazed at the ornate design etched onto Dae's back. He traced it reverently. "It's stunning," he murmured. "I was right. This bird—" he touched the raven and he swore it rustled its wings—"was not on this branch the last time I saw it."

There was a muffled snort from where Dae had buried his face. "It has a life of its own. It's the brand I'm forced to wear as the Djinn, representing all that is changeable and fleeting."

Ben charted the tree and its branches softly. "Did it hurt?"

Dae shook his head. "No. It was done magically, thank Shura. It tingled a bit, though."

Ben kissed down the centre of Dae's spine and his lover shivered in pleasure. "Well, let me take a little time to worship it." He reached

Dae's butt cheek and bit into it, not too gently. Dae startled and pushed his backside into the air.

"If you're hungry and need to eat something, I have a suggestion…"

Ben smiled as he parted Dae's cheeks and marvelled at the sight before him. "Now that's an invitation to dine I can't refuse."

***

Dae awoke to the sound of someone snoring in his ear. He was also being squashed by something or someone. He opened his eyes groggily as a furry tail swashed into his face, followed by a lick. He shot upright, registering the smell of dog breath.

"Ew, Tess," he sputtered, trying hard not to think where the dog's mouth had been. "You great lump of shoodlepopper, get off me this instant." All he got was another lick, and he uttered an "oof" as Tess changed position and plopped down on his legs.

"You won't move her," Ben said sleepily from his position under his pillow. "She moved in last night and even I can't get her to vacate the premises." He chuckled as Dae reached out and tried to move the heavy lump off his feet with an annoyed grunt.

"Well, I'm not having it," Dae grumbled. "I mean, how's a man supposed to lie in with this furry beast staking its claim?" He huffed and wriggled his legs from under the dog's bulk. "Now I'm awake. I may as well get up and have a pee." He looked at Tess hopefully. Perhaps he could trick the beast into going outside to do her business then he could get back into bed and close the door. "Need to go outside for a bit, Tess?" he wheedled. "It's not too cold out there." He glanced outside the window and shivered. *It looks fucking freezing.*

Tessa blinked at him with her big chocolate brown eyes and settled more comfortably onto the bed.

"I take it that's a no." Ben chuckled. "Looks like you'll be getting up or finding a way to get back into bed with her here, babe." He snuggled back under the duvet and Dae stared at him. The casual way Ben had said "babe" left him reeling. Dae wasn't sure whether it had slipped out because Ben was half asleep or whether it was something else.

He left Ben and Tess sleeping as he shuffled naked to the bathroom, shut the door, and sat down on the toilet seat.

Wasn't "babe" something people called someone in a relationship, meant for a person you truly care about? Dae knew Ben liked him—last night proved that—but oh frinx, what did it all mean?

The seat was cold under his backside so Dae stood up, took care of his business, then got into the shower. Once he'd done sprucing himself up, he went back into the bedroom. Ben was still asleep, Tess curled up next to him. Dae sighed. He'd fancied a little more hanky-panky this morning with his sexy bed-mate, but it seemed he'd been cockblocked by a dog. He scowled at Tess as he got dressed.

"Bad dog," he said softly, because after all, he didn't want to wake Ben. The man looked so delicious when he slept. Tess ignored him and farted. Dae wafted a hand in front of his nose. "Ye Gods, dog. That stinks. I'm out of here."

***

Curled up in Ben's favourite chair, a steaming cup of chamomile tea in hand, Dae contemplated his current situation. He'd been on earth for over a week and Ben didn't seem any closer to making his wishes. He hadn't even mentioned them, other than the unfortunate incident last night when he'd tried to send poor Rory to Puerto Rico. Dae snickered. He should be glad Ben felt that way about him, even if it was making life a little awkward emotion-wise. Dae had a feeling that was why his magic on Earth was reacting the way it was. His emotions were linked somehow and draining him of energy, more than it ever had before. Back in the lamp, and in Quimaria, there'd always been plenty of residual magic to top up on.

"What do I do?" he asked the squirrel outside, who was rooting in the grass for fallen acorns. "Do I press him to make the wishes and leave this place, or do I wait a bit longer and risk getting my heart broken again?"

Dae knew himself. He was in danger of falling hard for Ben.

Ben with the deep blue eyes, cheeky grin, and sweet soul, which took Dae's breath away. Any man who loved animals the way Ben did couldn't have a mean bone in his body.

The squirrel didn't answer, and ran up a tree and disappeared. Dae watched it go with a sigh. Sooner or later he'd get subliminal messages from Lady Mage Elincia politely asking him when he was going back to Calado'r. Other people may need wishes granted. Dae wasn't sure how long he could get away with delaying his return.

"If people don't give me their wishes, then what am I supposed to do?" he grumbled. He sipped his tea and looked out across the meadow contemplatively. Last time, his wish recipient couldn't wait to tell him what she wanted. Ben was stalling and while Dae now knew it was because of their connection, the time would come when he'd have to push Ben to give him his wishes.

Perhaps he could make some suggestions, get Ben on track. Heartened by the idea of channelling Ben's secret desires, Dae settled in to read his book and wait for Ben to get up. They could spend a lazy Sunday at home, perhaps with some home-cooked food and a good bottle of wine, then—who knew?

Perhaps Dae's unsuccessful attempt to get Ben into his clutches again could be realized to a successful conclusion.

Chapter 11

The strident ring of his mobile startled Ben out of a dream he'd been having, involving him, Dae, and a certain part of Dae's anatomy. He rolled over and picked up his phone from the bedside table.

Beside him, Dae mumbled something that sounded like "poxy son of a troll," then threw the duvet over his head again with a twist of his elegant arm. He'd taken to sleeping in Ben's bed almost every night because he "needed Ben's inert energy" while he slept to boost his magic.

Ben thought that was an excuse, but he wasn't going to argue. Being a human battery was kind of fun.

He squinted at his phone and frowned as he answered. "Alison? What's wrong?" It was three in the morning and Ben knew with a sense of dread the vet wouldn't be calling him unless there was a dire reason.

"Ben? I'm so sorry to call you, but we have a bit of an emergency. Honey's not well. I've been called out to see her, and Ben…" her voice choked up, "it's not looking good."

Ben swung his legs over the side of the bed and sat up, switching on his bedside light. "What kind of situation are we talking about?" In her basket in the corner of the room, Tess opened her eyes and stared at him groggily, then huffed and went back to sleep.

She was quiet for a few seconds then said, "Aspergillosis. I'm not a hundred percent sure but the symptoms are there."

Ben's heart sunk when he'd heard her words. Aspergillosis was a common avian disease of note: a fungal infection that could lead to death if not treated quickly. While not contagious from bird to bird, it meant that the rest of the colony might be infected with spores from the source and they'd need to be quarantined.

He stood and rummaged around for his clothes. As he pulled on his jeans, hopping from one leg to the other to stay balanced, Dae sat up, blinking sleepily.

"What's wrong? Are you going somewhere?"

Ben nodded. "There's a problem with one of the birds at the zoo. Remember Honey, the annoying bird who never does what she's told? She may have aspergillosis."

Dae blinked. "Asper what now?"

Ben pulled on his tee-shirt and looked around for his jumper. From the sound of the wind against the windows, it was cold out there. "It's a fungal disease in birds. It shouldn't be something we see at the zoo because we're damned careful about how we look after them. But that doesn't mean it's completely eradicated. Shit, where's my fucking jumper?"

He swore as he stubbed his toe on the foot of the bed. *Shit, that hurt.* Something soft hit him across the back of his head. His jumper. Ben turned around to see Dae's sympathetic gaze. His lover stood naked beside the bed and even in his current state of angst, Ben could appreciate Dae's lithe body.

"Thanks." He pulled on the warm bit of clothing and picked up his phone. "I need to get off to the zoo. I'll let you know how it goes." Even as he said the words, Ben marvelled he had someone he could say that to. He'd been so long on his own. It was rather a novelty having someone to call and give an update. Even if it were an otherworldly Djinn who would no doubt soon be going back to his own palatial home.

"Drive safely," Dae murmured. "I hope your bird is going to be all right. With you looking after him, she has a good chance."

"Thanks," Ben said gruffly. "See you later."

He jogged out of the bedroom, picked up his keys from the kitchen table, and was soon speeding his way towards Honey.

***

When Ben barrelled into the vet surgery, Alison looked at him gratefully. The surgery was warm, the antiseptic and musky animal scent hitting Ben's nostrils. It was a familiar, comforting smell, and Ben tried to smile at the vet as he walked over to the table where

Honey lay. She peered at him with bleary eyes and there was no sign of the troublemaking penguin Ben knew and loved.

"Glad you could come." Alison reached out and patted Honey's flank. "She's holding her own. I'm waiting for some tests back from my colleague, but I'm scared for her. She's not eating, she's listless, and struggling to breathe. Look at that." She pointed to Honey's beak. "Open-mouthed, trying to get air."

Ben stroked the bird's feathers gently, letting his long-time nemesis know he was there. "Sounds like it could be aspergillosis. How the heck did it happen *here*? We make sure their husbandry is suitable. We meet all the requirements to avoid this sort of disease."

Alison shrugged helplessly. "Things can happen. Bad luck, I guess. I've had all the other birds moved into the spare enclosure for the night. They weren't too happy, I can tell you. Poor Adam had his job cut out for him." Adam was Alison's assistant, a young vet learning the ropes. "I think Honey got a good peck of disapproval in."

Ben snorted. "She would, bloody little troublemaker. That's a good sign, though, right?" He leaned in and whispered to Honey. "Come on, sweetheart. Stay strong." His chest ached at seeing the usually rambunctious bird lying on the table. Honey blinked and looked at Ben sadly.

"You're going to be all right," Ben murmured, though he wasn't so sure. The disease, if it was what they suspected, had a high mortality rate.

Alison walked over to the ever-bubbling coffee machine on the side counter and poured them both a strong cup of black coffee. "Sorry, all out of milk. Sugar's in the bowl there if you need it."

Ben spooned two sugars into his mug and took a sip. He grimaced. "Jesus, how long has that been brewing? Tastes like tar."

His friend chuckled. "Adam made it earlier. He tends to have a heavy hand with the coffee grounds. I'd hate him to mix me an alcoholic drink."

For a moment, the two drank their coffee and regarded the quiet bird on the table.

"If it is aspers, we'll need a miracle to get her through it," Alison observed softly. "She was already a little immunocompromised, and this could be something she can't fight off. Antifungals may help, and we can give her some intravenous fluids and force-feed her fish gruel by tube if necessary."

Ben shuddered at the thought of the stout penguin resembling something out of a sci-fi film, filled with tubes and monitors. A glimmer of hope struck him.

"I may know someone who can help with a miracle," he said, then bit his lip because, honestly, he didn't want to have to explain the presence of a magic genie in his life. He'd be carted off in a straitjacket.

Alison looked hopeful. "Oh, who?"

"Erm, a specialist I know. He may have some advice. I'll give him a call." Ben plonked his mug on the counter and walked into the small office at the back of the surgery. This was a call he couldn't afford anyone to overhear.

At home, the phone rang, over and over again. "Come on, Dae, pick up," he entreated. The man had probably gone back to bed. Well, this was an emergency and Ben was sure the genie could cope with it for one night. "Pick up, you bastard."

There was a click and Dae's voice came over the line. "If you're trying to fucking sell me anything at this time of night, I will—"

Ben didn't have time to hear one of Dae's rather creative curses. "It's me," he said urgently. "I want to make a wish."

"A wish? What kind of wish?" Dae asked, sounding apprehensive. Ben took a deep breath.

"Oh Djinn of the lamp, please grant me my wish. I want Honey the penguin to be healed from what ails her and restored to full health." Ben waited for the confirmation of his wish, not expecting to hear Dae's deep sigh of regret.

"Oh Ben, that won't work at all. I'm sorry."

Ben's stomach dropped. "What the fuck do you mean, it won't work? You have to grant me my wish. That's what I want." Anger built in his chest at being denied.

There was a short silence on the other end of the phone. When Dae finally spoke, his tone was compassionate. "Ben, when we first met, I told you one of the things we Djinns can't do is heal. I don't have the power to do what you ask of me."

"Why the hell not? This is my mate, Dae. She's a mom and she doesn't deserve to have a lingering death, unable to breathe. I need her to get better."

"I can't. I would do it in a heartbeat if it were within my remit, but matters of life and death, sickness and health, are not one of them. I'm so sorry." Dae's voice caught. "I understand you're upset but—"

"Oh, I get it," Ben spat into the phone, catching another glimpse of Honey in the surgery. "You can grant frivolous wishes to aspiring actresses and wannabe Hollywood stars, but when it comes to the serious, really meaningful stuff, you're hopeless. What's the point of having a genie if they can't grant the one thing you really want?" He tightened his grip around his mobile.

He heard Dae draw a deep breath. "Ben, that's not fair. I was clear when I told you what was and wasn't within my powers to grant. I've never misled you or promised anything I couldn't deliver."

"Well, I'd have thought that as my lover of the aeon, and the man you owe something to, you'd make an exception. Guess I'm not as special after all." Ben heard the bitterness in his tone. He wasn't usually prone to drama, but…this was Honey. Defiant mischief-maker of the enclosure and mother to one other little penguin called Taffy.

Dae didn't reply but Ben heard his soft breaths. He felt a little guilty going off at Dae as he had, but what was the point of having magic if it couldn't be used to do good for an ailing animal?

"I hope your bird pulls through, Ben," Dae said quietly. "I shall continue to channel positive thoughts from my side." The call went dead.

Ben stared at his mobile in frustration. Now what? A face peered in at him from the doorway. Adam stood there, his freckled face ruddy under a thatch of ginger hair.

"Alison told me to tell you the results of the tests will still be a while. She wanted to know if you wanted any more coffee?"

Ben grimaced. "No thanks, I value my stomach." He tried to grin at Adam to take the sting out of his words. "Tell her I'll be there in a bit."

Adam nodded and disappeared. Ben slumped down in the desk chair and laid his head on his arms. Damn and blast. Now he was sure he'd pissed Dae off. He did vaguely remember Dae telling him the rules back at the beginning, but in truth, he'd not listened to them much, being so surprised at having a mystical being in his house.

What the hell am I going to do now?

***

Back home, in bed, Dae sat in darkness, trying to calm his rapidly beating heart. Ben's pain had seeped through the phone and Dae understood it all too well. The pain of losing something you loved was agonising, whether it was the love of your life or an animal you had a lot of affection for. No one had a monopoly on it, and it snuck in at the most inopportune times.

Dae felt useless in the face of Ben's entreaty and he wished he could grant the wish. Tess had jumped up on the bed with him and Dae stroked her warm fur as he mused.

"He was angry, Tess," Dae murmured to the dog. "And so hurt." His chest ached with compassion. Being a Djinn might have been a punishment, but it was his current lot in life and he tried to make a proper job of it. Being accused of not taking it seriously wounded him.

Tess snuffled and licked Dae's hand. "Doggy kisses for me? Thank you." Dae patted Tess's head. He'd grown quite fond of the lazy mutt to the point he didn't mind her drool on his hands. "Your owner is a bit of a douchebag, you know that?" He huffed as he settled back in bed. Tess, as anticipated, stretched out beside him, taking up most of the space. "Tess, move that fat behind of yours. Now. There's two of us in this bed, you know."

Tess grumbled but moved around, leaving Dae able to pull the blankets around him as he lay down. "That's better, you bed hog." He closed his eyes but every time he did, he heard Ben's angry voice saying he wasn't as special as he'd thought he was.

How wrong you are, Dae thought with a pang. *You're special to me, Ben Sinclair. I wish you weren't, but it seems once again I've fallen for the wrong man. These wonderful times we've had together will soon stop and I'll be going back home.*

He had to have a conversation soon about Ben's wishes—or rather, the lack thereof. These last two weeks was the longest Dae had ever spent on Earth to grant wishes, and he knew sooner or later, he'd have to insist on Ben using them. Lady Mage Elicia would be starting to get impatient, and of course, somewhere out there was another person with wishes to grant. The lamp needed to move on.

This time, though, Dae thought with a pang, things were different. He loved this world, he lov—liked Ben, and while Earth was filled with humans who never ceased to surprise Dae with the depths of their frailty and mistakes, they were also kind and compassionate. The ones who tried to make the world a better place outnumbered those who didn't.

"I could be happy here," Dae muttered drowsily to Tess as she snuffled in her sleep. "I truly could."

***

Dae woke up to the sound of a coffee grinder, a raucous sound that shattered his sleep and assaulted his ears. He groaned and pulled the pillow over his head, trying to drown out the racket.

"Honestly, this early in the morning?" He peered blearily at the clock and blinked. Oh, not that early. It was already ten am. He frowned. If the noise was Ben, and he hoped to God it was and not some serial killer grinding coffee beans, then why wasn't Ben at work? He looked beside him and sighed. It seemed Ben hadn't graced him again with his presence last night. He'd probably slept on the couch. Dae sighed. It was the most uncomfortable place he knew to sleep on. Ben must be both knackered and aching. *Serves him right.*

Dae clambered out of bed, pulled on a soft pair of joggers and a matching sweatshirt, and marched into the kitchen. He'd brush his teeth and have a shower later. He found Ben making coffee from the grounds he'd noisily prepared, no doubt a move to irritate Dae.

"Good morning," Dae said deferentially. He'd be the bigger man this morning and make the first overture, even though he dreaded the answer. "How is Honey?"

"Better, no thanks to you," Ben grunted. He was bare-chested, wearing only a loose pair of jogging bottoms that highlighted his spectacular arse.

Dae raised an eyebrow. So this was how it was going to be then? Fine. He could be as dramatic as the next person. Indeed, he had many degrees in drama and was the most dramatic-ist person who ever lived. Ben Sinclair was so going to lose at this game.

"That's wonderful news. Was it what you suspected?" Dae watched as Ben took his coffee cup over to the kitchen island and sat down on a stool. *I suppose I'll have to make my own coffee.* Tut-tutting under his breath, but loud enough for Ben to hear, Dae made a great show out of getting a cup and making his drink. Ben wasn't the only one who could employ churlish antics.

"No. It was a false alarm, thank God. The tests came back negative. It was something else, a bacterial infection. Alison has her on antibiotics and says she should recover." Ben pulled the morning newspaper towards him and spread it open, reading as he sipped his coffee.

"Excellent. I'm glad she's going to be well." Dae poked at the newspaper and Ben looked up, scowling. "Anything interesting in there?" No answers. "Aren't you supposed to be at work?"

"Alison and I have the day off. We got home about seven am." He ran his head through his hair. "I'm reading the sports page. Know anything about rugby?" Ben cocked a challenging brow at Dae, who nodded enthusiastically.

"Oh yes. Big men in tight shorts with hefty arms. What's not to like?" He shivered. "And that thing they do when they all get together and huddle while touching each other's backsides…I find it rather a turn-on."

Ben's lips twitched, and with a sense of satisfaction, Dae knew he was trying to hold back a smile.

"There's more to rugby than beefy blokes." Ben continued to read his paper and Dae moved it once again. "What do you want now?" Ben growled. "Can't a man read his paper in peace?"

Dae pursed his lips. "I heard there was a funfair in town." It wasn't a lie, there *was* a fair in town. Dae had seen the flyers plastered all over the shop windows. There was also one on the bottom of the page Ben was currently reading. "I thought perhaps we could go there on the weekend. I love funfairs." He pursed his lips. "You're not going to talk to me at all, or for a while?"

The fleeting wince on Ben's forehead mollified Dae somewhat. It seemed Ben was at least a little sorry about his harsh comments last night.

"Don't be such a cock," muttered Ben. "Of course I'm going to talk to you."

Dae ignored him, pretending to read the news over Ben's shoulder. A shoulder that appeared to be aching given the amount of rolling and rubbing Ben was doing to it.

"I saw you didn't come back to bed last night when you got home," Dae said. "Were you too late? I wouldn't have minded. You could have woken me."

"I didn't want to disturb you. I crashed on the couch for a couple of hours then had to get up for a bloody pee." He shrugged. "I thought I might as well stay up for now."

"Sleep well then, did you? I notice you're rubbing your shoulder." Dae sat back, his final repartee in place. *There's no point in antagonising the man any further. My work is done.*

Ben ignored him but Dae noticed his hand drop away from the aching shoulder to frame his paper instead. Dae stood up and pecked a kiss on the top of Ben's head. "I am glad your bird is better," he said softly. "I know how much she means to you. All those animals have a special place in your heart. You're a good man, Ben Sinclair."

"Yeah, well, we were lucky it was nothing worse." Ben pushed the newspaper aside and looked up at Dae standing with his hips leaning against the kitchen sink. "I'm sorry I went off the handle with you this morning," he said gruffly. "I was worried about Honey. I shouldn't have said what I did."

Dae waved a hand, relieved by the apology. "Consider it forgotten. Humans have a way of emoting that sometimes makes no sense, but it's an endearing trait most of the time."

"Of course we can go to the funfair. I like them too," Ben muttered.

Dae grinned. "Wonderful. We had them all the time in Calado'r and my homeland. Wonderful affairs with lights everywhere, attractions that take your breath away, and magic sparking everywhere. I spent a lot of time in them as a child."

Ben snorted. "Don't get your hopes up for ours. The best you'll get is a soggy hot dog, cotton candy that'd make your teeth rot, kids running around misbehaving, and the local lads starting a fight."

Dae shook his head sadly. "Trust you to take all the fun out of it. Surely there must be something you enjoy, something you loved doing as a child?"

Ben cocked his head. "The Haunted House. I loved riding the train through the dark, seeing what was coming out to scare us. I knew they weren't real, but every time they jumped out, I screamed. Good times."

Dae wasn't sure what was so fun about being scared to death, but he'd be prepared to suffer it if it made Ben happy. And maybe, just maybe, he could conjure up an extra-special something in there for Ben, to make his evening. He hugged that thought to himself and smiled.

"Then it's a date. Cotton Candy Tooth Destroyer, here we come."

Chapter 12

Ben was right. The local funfair was nothing like those held at home, but Dae thought it was passable. The park grounds were filled with stalls and attractions spiked with flickering fairy lights and rambunctious flashing ones. On the Big Wheel to his right, people viewed the countryside from up high, and the strange bullet-shaped contraption currently spinning crazily to the accompaniment of people screaming and begging to get off accompanied the hustle and bustle of the customers packing the grounds.

Even the weather was cooperating.

Dae plunged his hand into his buttered popcorn and stuffed another load into his mouth. Beside him, Ben stood close, grinning at the delight Dae was taking in his salty treat.

"That's your second box," he murmured. "Where the hell are you putting it all?"

Dae chewed happily and sauntered over to another stall selling round, sticky red things on sticks. "These look tasty," he remarked. "What are they?"

"Sticky toffee apples." Ben gestured to the woman behind the stall to hand him one, then drew a few coins out of his pocket to pay her. "Here, try one."

Dae eyed the treat greedily. "Here, hold this," he commanded and gave his popcorn box to Ben. He sniffed the toffee apple, then took a huge bite out of it. His mouth was flooded with hardened sugar, spiced with the taste and texture of apples. He wasn't a fan. The apple was okay but the toffee wasn't his favourite. He grimaced and handed the confection back to Ben, taking his treasured popcorn back. "Here, you can have that. It's a bit too sweet for me."

He stared around the funfair. "So, where's this Haunted House thing you like? Maybe we can take a ride on it." In front of them, a child screamed in happiness as she was handed a rotund hippo in reward for apparently knocking a bunch of balls off a rack.

Ben took Dae's hand and tugged him forward. "Come on, I'll show you. It's usually on the far side of the field, where the lights are lower. Sets the atmosphere, you know?"

Dae was pulled along through the throngs of people to the back of the park. The lights grew dimmer as they neared what looked like a large dwelling bearing the words "The Ghoulish Grotto." As they got closer, Ben stopped, standing in the queue. He continued to hold Dae's hand, and feeling Ben's strong fingers laced with his warmed him.

"It shouldn't be a long wait. It's a pretty popular ride." Ben grinned. "I promise you can hold on to me if you get scared. Don't be embarrassed." He winked.

Dae thought that if you'd camped in the Screaming Forest of Quimaria for a night, and encountered a terrifying, tentacled Badooberong, nothing could scare you, but he let Ben have his assumption a screaming Dae was going to cling to him. Nothing like a great excuse to get closer. Perhaps even to share a little sexy hanky-panky as they travelled the route.

Five minutes into the ride, Dae was yawning with boredom. He hadn't seen one thing yet that gave him the faintest opportunity to cling onto Ben. Bedraggled papier-mâché puppets on obvious strings fell from the ceiling, and canned screams and gibbering ghostly noises echoed through the cavernous chamber.

Honestly, Dae thought dispiritedly, it was enough to put the evil villains of the world to shame. What in frinx name were these humans thinking charging a whole three pounds each for the privilege of being assaulted by badly made skeletons and smelly obnoxious gases? It was an insult. He needed to put this right, starting now.

Beside him, Ben laughed wildly as a tatty witch swung down from the ceiling and brushed his face with cobwebs.

Right, that's it. That thing is damned pathetic. Ben deserves more than this. I'll give you all your monies' worth.

Dae closed his eyes and summoned his magic. The prickling in his fingers built as he drew forth enchantments from his stifled reservoir. He may not be as powerful here, but son of a sea cook, he could still cast an epic spell. Mumbling to himself under his breath, he gathered his forces together then with a simple flick of his fingers, he shot it forth into the dark ahead. Pleased with himself, he sat back to enjoy the fun.

The first inkling he had something was wrong when the bloodcurdling screams from one of the cars in front began. Truly, those screams were the scariest thing Dae had experienced so far tonight.

Ben grabbed his hand tightly. "What the fuck is that? Are those real people screaming, or part of the ride?" His voice trailed off as a nightmare of a creature slunk around the bend in front of their car. Dae knew it was merely mist and would dissipate within minutes—to be replaced by another equally fearsome creature—but it was still a loathsome sight. Resembling a combination of black horned goat and salamander, it padded forwards on lizard appendages, tossing its horns, looking about to disembowel someone. Its scaly tail swiped from side to side as it made a noise similar to the sounds of Ben grinding coffee beans in the morning.

Ben let out a screech and Dae's fingers almost cracked under the pressure of his hand in his. "Jesus fuck, what the hell is that thing? It is part of the show, right? Please tell me it's part of the show." His breath quickened and even in the darkness, Dae saw Ben's eyes wide open in fear.

"Of course it's part of the ride. What else would it be? I mean, those people seem to be enjoy—" His voice trailed off as the people in the front two carts bailed out, shouting and screaming, and attempted to bash the creature's head in with what looked like a lady's handbag and a steel flask. Of course, the items passed through the apparition and soon there were only trails of green and black smoke and tendrils of blue wafting through the air. There was a temporary hiatus as the onlookers stood about in stunned incomprehension, then the screaming started again as something else was spotted clambering across the ceiling.

"Perhaps the hellhound was a tad ambitious," Dae muttered to himself as the animal snarled and launched itself at one of the patrons, a young man in a parka and jeans, who seemed rooted to the spot in fear. As the hellhound landed on his head, the man fell to the floor in a faint. Everyone else ran towards Dae and Ben, shoving past them in a paroxysm of terror. No doubt they thought they were headed for the entrance.

Dae wasn't sure they were going the right way. He rather thought they might be heading into the bowels of the ride, where—ahem and alas—more visions awaited them.

Ben sprang out of the car and ran over to the fallen man. "Dae, give me a hand to get him back into the car. Hopefully, they'll start moving again soon and we can get him out of here."

They managed to get the unconscious man into the seat of his ride and clambered in beside him. Both behind and ahead of them, there were still sounds of terror and shrieks as people encountered more of Dae's creations.

Horsefeathers. Perhaps I should retract the enchantments before they kill someone with a heart attack. Dae flexed his fingers and muttered the words to stop the carnage spreading through the funfair. The hellhound disappeared around the bend and Dae hoped it had gone for good. Sometimes these mischievous things had a mind of their own. He blinked his sudden fatigue away.

I have a headache. I need to lie down.

"Wait until I get out of here," Ben said darkly. "The owner of this damned place is going to get a fucking mouthful. I'm all for a scary ghost ride, but this went too far."

Dae squinted at him in confusion mixed with some apprehension. Ben sounded rather fierce. "I thought the whole idea of these things was to be scared?"

Ben scowled. "Yes, but there's a difference between scared by a stupid fair show, where you know more or less what's coming, and being terrified by slavering monsters that get up close and personal."

Dae would never understand the way the human mind worked. Suddenly, the cart jerked and moved forward.

"At last," Ben muttered. "We can get out of here and I can have words."

Dae wasn't sure how he was going to protect the unfortunate ride manager from Ben's wrath without admitting his part in the unfortunate affair. That was something he wasn't looking forward to explaining.

"Are you all right?" Ben asked. "That was *some* experience for your first haunted house ride."

Dae nodded. "I'm fine, I've got a bit of a headache." He looked over at the man slumped in the chair. "I'm sorry he collapsed. Is it serious, do you think?"

Ben shook his head. "No, his pulse is good. I think he fainted. He'll be fine once we get out into the fresh air."

The cart with its burden of three grown men rattled along the train line, and finally Dae saw flashing lights at the exit to the tunnel he'd caused chaos in. His stomach churned when he realised he would have to face the music outside. *That* was something he wasn't looking forward to. At all.

As the cart wobbled out into the light-spangled night, he noticed with some discomfort a group of people gathering. They were all gesticulating wildly and pointing towards the tunnel.

"I tell you, it's proper haunted," one excited teenager in a hoodie proclaimed. "Mate, you wouldn't believe what we saw in there."

An older woman clinging to the arm of a man, probably her husband, nodded her head fervently. "I've never experienced anything like that in my life. My brother," she waved to a man on the ground sitting with an asthma inhaler pressed to his mouth, "he should sue you for causing him an asthma attack. We all should. It was absolutely terrifying."

Oh frinx and double frinx, Dae groaned silently. This was worse than he thought. A sudden perk of optimism took hold of him. Perhaps he could make everyone forget about the event? It was magic he hadn't tried before, and it would no doubt leave him feeling even more nauseous and tired, but it might be worth the effort. Especially if he didn't have to tell Ben about his part in the situation.

A fiercer headache may be worth it.

Before he could carry through with his plan, he became aware of Ben impatiently tugging his arm.

"Come on, Dae. Give me a hand to get this poor bloke over to the medical tent. It's over there, not far." Dae found himself lifting the now half-conscious man over to a waiting employee, who rushed forward to take the man off their hands.

"He fainted inside," Ben offered as he looked around, eyes wide at the commotion. "Something went wrong in there and everyone got a bit more fright than they bargained for."

Dae cleared his throat. "Perhaps we should go, leave them to sort it out. We don't want to get in the way." Instead of performing magic, perhaps they could simply leave, and forget this had ever happened.

Before Ben could reply, a tall, bull-headed man stormed forward and bellowed at the top of his voice. He was about six foot ten, as wide as a sumo wrestler, and covered in tattoos. "I don't know what the 'ell you all are talkin' about. I'm never put anything like what you saw in my ride. It's the same way it's always been. If anyone fucked with my ride, it wasn't me." He glared around at the crowd, who'd all gone strangely silent. "Now have any of you people got any evidence to prove that something caused all this bloody fuss? 'Cause if you do, I'd like to see it."

The crowd muttered and one of the young people who'd been on the ride shrugged. "It all happened too fast and the damn things didn't stay around long enough for me to get a picture. It all disappeared. Like a puff of smoke, it was."

Dae began to feel hopeful that he may not have to invoke his talents after all. "Come on, Ben, let's go get some of that delicious mulled wine over there. I fancy a quick something to eat too, don't you? Those German sausage thingies look tasty."

Ben swivelled, turning to face him. His eyes narrowed. "You seem a bit too eager to leave," he muttered. "Is there something I should know?"

Faced with what appeared to be Ben's increasing suspicion, Dae's nerves were shot.

"What?" he asked, wide-eyed himself. "No, never. I'm an open book, nothing to see here." He giggled nervously. "Did you hear that? My stomach is growling. I need to eat."

Ben passed a hand over his eyes, then looked at Dae in consternation. "Dae, what the fuck did you do?"

Dae deflated under Ben's withering gaze. "Fine," he muttered. "I tried to make the ride more interesting for you because you seemed so taken with it. How was I supposed to know everyone would get so damned scared at a few apparitions? I thought the whole idea of the thing was to be scared, so honestly, you can't blame me for giving them what they wanted."

"You what?" Ben's strangled groan sounded painful. "Oh my God. I don't believe this." He took a quick, panicked look around. "Come on. We need to get away from here. I need a drink."

"That's exactly what I've been saying," Dae grumbled as he was dragged away towards a brightly lit tent offering beer and wine. "How come when you say it, it's okay?"

Ben said nothing as he headed straight for the makeshift bar and raised two fingers at the barmaid. "Two beers please." He drummed his fingers impatiently on the bar top while glancing around nervously.

"I don't think anyone followed us in here," Dae said snappily. "Can we please order something to eat? I'm starving."

The barmaid handed over their beers and Ben paid her, then shepherded Dae over to a small, empty corner table. "I'll go get us some burgers next door," he said. "Wait here. Don't bloody move. You've done enough damage for one night." He flounced out of the tent entrance—or was it an exit when the opening did both—and Dae huffed a discontented sigh.

Really, what on earth was all the fuss about? "You try to add a little spice to your boyfriend's life and what does he do, he—" Dae froze as he played back what he'd said. Boyfriend? *Boyfriend?* Oh dear. This wasn't good. This wasn't good at all.

He was still sitting there pondering this new turn of events when Ben came back with two delicious, fully stacked hamburgers wrapped in tinfoil.

"Looks like the panic has gone down a bit out there. People still swear they saw supernatural entities, but the ride manager isn't being blamed anymore. Business is booming. There was a queue a mile long of muppets waiting to go in. Go figure."

Dae fell upon his food like a ravenous wolf and pushed all thoughts of anything else from his mind. Eat first, reflect second.

"Tell me why you decided to create havoc at the fairground," Ben asked as he wiped mustard off his mouth. Dae would have liked to lick it off, but something told him that might be going a little too far. "You said something about wanting to make it more interesting…for me."

Dae wiped crumbs off his lips and shrugged. "You said you enjoyed these things, so I wanted to make it special. You deserve it."

Ben reached over and took Dae's hand in his. "A lovely sentiment and I appreciate it. Thing is, maybe we should leave the special stuff for when we're alone at home?" His fingers stroked Dae's gently. Dae swallowed. Those sensuous gestures were causing havoc with his senses and his groin. He and Ben had fooled about a few times since Dae started sleeping in Ben's bed, but the last time had been two days ago.

"Ben, while we're talking about magic…" Dae took a deep breath. "We need to have a conversation about your wishes."

Ben immediately retracted his hand and scowled. "What *about* my wishes?"

Dae sighed. "I can't stay here forever. You know I have to go back sometime. If I don't at least grant *one* of your wishes, the Lady Mage will arrive here personally to encourage me. She can be quite fearsome."

Ben's lips tightened. "Will you be punished?"

Dae shook his head. "I don't believe so. Djinns are given fairly free rein on their wish-granting, but I've been here nearly two weeks. They'll start to ask questions."

Ben toyed with his beer bottle. "So I'd better get to it and make a wish then." He smiled, a twisted thing that made Dae wince. "So you can go home."

Those last flat words made Dae's heart ache. "It's not that I'm anxious to go. You know that. I like being with you. But I'm a Djinn and I have…responsibilities." *I'd rather stay here with you. If you wanted me enough.*

Ben raised his empty bottle in a mocking cheer. "Then I guess I should get serious and think about what I want." He grinned fleetingly. "I think I know already." He stood up. "Now, come on. I promised you a ride on the Big Wheel. Let's get up there and I can show you the countryside from up high. It's spectacular."

He dashed out of the tent, leaving Dae staring after him.

After a few moments, Dae stood and followed him out into the cool night towards the flickering lights of the illuminated wheel.

Chapter 13

"Isn't he a cutie?" Ben watched Taffy swimming around. Dae stood next to him in the enclosure. Given the delighted noises the Djinn was making, he was charmed by the penguin's antics.

"He's so damned cute," Dae enthused as he tossed another sprat to the colony of penguins sunning themselves on the rocks. "Are they always this greedy?"

Ben chuckled. "Yep. You're their best friend right now." He threw more food their way, and the ones in the water dived elegantly to retrieve it. The zoo had closed for the evening ten minutes ago. Ben thought it would be a treat to take Dae to see his treasured animals outside of the hoo-ha of the usual visiting times.

"Tell me more about penguins," Dae asked as he put down the now empty sprat container and perched his behind on a rock. The sun was low in the sky but there was enough sunshine to warm them as they loitered. "Why do they look as if they're wearing a tuxedo?" His eyes sparkled in the waning sunlight as he stretched his longs legs out in front of him and drew his long jumper sleeves over his hands, which looked a little blue. He looked relaxed and quite adorable.

Ben laughed. "It's called countershading and it's pretty clever. When they're swimming in the water, from the top they look dark to predators above, like they're part of the ocean. From below, the white of their bellies blends in with the sun, distracting predators below. It's a camouflage tactic used not only by penguins but sharks, dolphins, porpoises, even insects." He shrugged. "Land animals have it too, like deer. It's nature's way of protecting certain species."

"Wow, fascinating." Dae cocked an eyebrow. "They swallow the fish whole. Don't they have teeth to chew with?"

Ben shook his head. "No teeth. Instead, they have these weird fleshy things—we call them spines—on the inside of their mouths, which face backwards. They allow the fish to slide easier into the gullet."

Ben was gratified to notice Dae looked well impressed at his knowledge. He hadn't spent years at university and researching abroad to not know his subject matter. He didn't get a chance to show it off much.

"Penguins can drink seawater too. You'll see them sipping it. They have a gland above their eye, called the supraorbital gland, which acts to remove the sodium chloride from their bloodstream. They excrete it through the bill, or by sneezing."

Dae's eyes bugged out. "Oh, how bizarre. Sneezing it out? That's different." He grimaced. "Remind me not to get close to them if that's ever going to happen. Penguin snot is not something I want to experience."

Ben saw him shiver and decided Penguin School was over. "Come on, let's go inside and I'll make us a hot chocolate. Then after that, I'll lock up and we can go home."

He shepherded Dae indoors and smiled when Dae breathed a sigh of relief at getting warmer. The sun was dipping below the horizon, and the air outside was cooling.

His sun-loving Djinn preferred the warmth, no doubt of that. Ben was looking forward to taking him on a trip to the coast when the summer came, perhaps having a sundowner at Ben's favourite pub on the beach in Devon while basking in the late afternoon sun.

Oh, wait. He put on the brakes on his thoughts. Dae wouldn't be around then, would he? He'd have granted Ben's wishes and gone home. Unless of course, Ben never made either of his wishes and kept Dae here with him.

I mean, how much trouble could he get into with this Lady Mage anyway? He already said he'd likely not be punished.

But that meant his first wish, the one he'd brought Dae here for tonight, wouldn't be granted and the benefactor he had in mind wouldn't receive the spoils. Ben couldn't be that selfish.

"Penny for them," Dae said softly, a quirky smile on his face. "Where did you go right then?"

Ben blinked, realising he was standing in the small staff kitchen with a small milk pan and nothing else. "Oh, nothing important.

Thinking about something I need to do tomorrow." He took a breath and opened the cupboard to locate the tin of hot chocolate, then found the milk. He sniffed it, decided it was still okay to use, and poured some in the saucepan.

Dae looked amused. "This seems like something you've done often," he remarked. "All the steps neatly coordinated, mugs ready, stove switched on. I take it this is a thing with you?" He leapt nimbly onto the countertop and sat there, legs swinging as he watched Ben prepare their drinks.

Ben nodded as he placed the milk pan on the heated stovetop plate. "We're all partial to hot chocolate, Hazel, me, and Hemmy. It's a bit of a stress reliever at the end of the day. Although I always seem to be the one making it," he grumbled. He pulled out a chair from around the small canteen table and sat down.

"You look so comfortable here, in this place." Dae looked around wistfully. "It's another home to you, isn't it? I can see why. Everyone I've met is so friendly and they make me feel so welcome." He rolled his eyes. "Even if I am only your cousin Dan from Scotland."

Ben sniggered. The ruse was still working and as Dae wasn't at the zoo that often, it was easy enough for him to slip into his Scottish persona. Only Ben—at least he hoped it was only him—noted the occasional lapse from the accent.

Hazel adored *Dan*, and the first time she'd met him, she'd plied him with stories of her trip to the Highlands on a Nessie exploration trip, giving a rather disgusting account of her first time eating black pudding, only to find out afterwards what it was made of. The resultant tale of woe and upchucking had made them all gag.

"Talking of this being my second home..." Ben fiddled with a spoon. "I've decided on my first wish."

Dae drew in a sharp breath. "Son of a beaver. You have?" He jumped down from the countertop. "That's...erm...wonderful." Ben thought he didn't sound all that enthused. He'd expected more delight at his decision. What was all that about?

"It's one involving money," Ben admitted. "You did say that was possible?" He'd given his wish a lot of thought, and he hoped he was approaching things the right way.

"Of course, I can make you as rich as you want." Dae sounded vaguely disappointed. "Jewels, bearer bonds, gold bullion, cash—anything you need."

"No, nothing like that. I want to put the cash into someone's bank account. How does that work exactly? I mean, do I need to give you the bank details or what?"

Dae chuckled. "Nothing like that. Magic, remember? You simply tell me what you want, how you want it, and poof. It happens. Even I don't have a clue as to the mechanics. All I know is that it works."

"Okay." Ben took a deep breath. "Here goes." He closed his eyes then opened them to ask, "Will there be a bright light, or a flash or something when you grant my wish?" *How cool would that be?*

"It's a wish. You're not dying, Ben," Dae said with dry amusement. "I sincerely hope you don't see a bright light. My advice? If you do, please don't go into it."

Ben scowled. "Don't be a sarky bastard. I've never done this before, all right?" He closed his eyes again and took a moment to ready himself before he started.

Then he began: "Oh Djinn of the lamp, please grant me my first wish. I would like the amount of one hundred thousand pounds transferred to the bank account of Windward Zoo. In Winchester. In England." He made sure to narrow down the zoo because who knew how these things worked? He didn't want it going to another Windward Zoo somewhere in the world.

Ben felt a puff of soft air wash over his face, mixed with the scent of sandalwood. He opened one eye carefully then gasped when he saw a swirl of rainbow colours, like a mystic portal, directly in front of him. Beside him, Dae stood, twirling his finger in a movement that echoed the swirly turns of the entity.

"Is this impressive enough for you?" Dae smirked as he whirled his finger faster. The kaleidoscope of colour made Ben's eyes water and he began to lose focus.

"Could you please stop doing that?" he said gruffly. "It's giving me a headache."

Dae huffed and lowered his hand. The portal dissipated into thin streaks of red, green, purple, and blue. "I thought you wanted a bit of a spectacle when you made your wish," he muttered. "Honestly, some people are hard to please."

Ben choked back a chuckle at Dae's fit of pique. God, the man was something else. "So what happens now?"

"Now?" Dae looked at him in surprise. "Nothing. It's done."

Ben blinked in confusion. "You mean, that's it? The money is in their account already?"

Dae sniffed. "Of course. There are no moths on me."

Ben burst out into a fit of laughter. Dae looked affronted. "I beg your pardon. Is it something I said?"

Ben nodded and tried to catch his breath. "It's not moths, it's flies. We say there are no flies on us when we want to impress people with how quick and clever we've been."

"Moths, flies, whatever." Dae flipped a finger at him in irritation. "You're welcome, by the way."

Ben moved over to him and drew Dae in for a hug. "Thank you, oh wise and wonderful Djinn. That money will mean so much to the zoo. Hazel has been doing amazing things with the little money she has, but this will go a long way towards repairing the enclosures and setting up the new monkey environments and more." He flushed. "I wasn't sure whether I should ask for more, but that seemed greedy. I mean, I don't know where the money's coming from, and I didn't want anyone else to lose out because of my wish."

"You British people are so polite and proper," Dae said with a fond smile. "I might have known your first wish would be for someone else," Dae murmured into Ben's throat. "You are a rare and incredible man, Ben Sinclair." The feel of Dae's form against him, his warm breath on Ben's skin, and the knowledge he'd been able to help a place he thought of as home lent warmth to Ben's body as he pulled Dae closer.

"Hazel won't be able to trace it back to me, will she? I want to remain anonymous."

Dae's lips brushed against Ben's cheek. "We've been doing this a while, and we know all the money rules. The money will reflect as a deposit from the Life Lottery of Benevolence, which is an internationally registered lottery organisation located offshore. Ergo, no tax. The winning lottery ticket will be in your desk drawer at home if anyone questions anything."

"Wow," Ben said, drunk on Dae's proximity and the seductive spicy scent he exuded. "You guys think of everything, don't you?"

Dae didn't answer, but took Ben's lips in a hard kiss, pressing him against the wall as his hands slid under Ben's shirt to rest on his skin. Ben opened his mouth to let Dae in and moaned softly as their tongues met, and Dae's warm fingers brushed against his nipples.

"God, you know how to push my buttons." Ben groaned as Dae's deft fingers unzipped his jeans and slid inside his boxers to cup his balls. "I could so get used to this."

Dae's mouth drew away and his purple gaze transfixed Ben with what looked like hope. "You could? Having me around, you mean, or the sex?"

"Both." Ben pulled Dae's enticing mouth back to his and pressed a fleeting kiss on his lips. "I love having you here."

Dae's soft smile grew wider. "I like being here," he affirmed as he caressed Ben's dick. Ben took in a sharp breath and melted against Dae's lithe body. "I feel I'm at home here, isn't that strange? I have worlds to choose from, yet not one pleases me as much as this one. It's all because you're in it."

Ben gave a fierce growl. "We need to move this to the staff room right now. There's a bed in there." *And no one will come in there to catch us in the act.* He released Dae and stepped back, only for his nose to twitch as something malodorous caught his attention.

"Mm, I think the milk is burning," Dae murmured with a grin. He sauntered over to the saucepan and clicked the hob dial off. He wrinkled his nose in distaste. "That's gonna be a bitch to clean. Looks like our hot chocolate is on hold for a while."

"Fuck the hot chocolate." Ben pulled Dae out of the kitchen and down the narrow hall. "I have other things I'd rather be doing right now."

"Me, you mean?" Dae purred sultrily. "About time. I have something else in mind for now," he whispered as they entered the staff room. "Something we haven't tried before. I think you'll enjoy it."

Ben's imagination went off the charts. Sex with Dae was always inventive and fun, and as sexy as hell. Ben's past partners had often jibed at him not wanting the whole anal sex thing. With Dae, that didn't seem to matter.

In between frantic kissing, rubbing, and moans of pleasure, they managed to undress each other and fall onto the narrow guest bed naked.

Dae immediately took over, kissing Ben's erogenous zones—his hip, the skin behind his ear, his collarbone. Ben lay sprawled beneath an insatiable man, one who took great delight in inciting every cell in Ben's body to flame.

The warmth of Dae's body, the soft entreaties he whispered in Ben's ear, and the rhythmic movements of his hips against Ben's most tender parts left Ben soaring to a place he never wanted to leave.

"Turn around," Dae murmured and Ben gasped as he did so, and Dae spooned him from behind.

"Relax, I'm not going inside you. I want you to feel me, *here*," Dae pressed at Ben's taint. "Is that all right?"

Ben nodded, unable to speak. He pushed back against Dae as Dae's cock slid between his cheeks, slick and heated, iron against flesh. Dae thrust unevenly for a while until they found their symphony, and between them, the delicious pressure of movements fitted together like instruments in an orchestra drove them both to a crescendo. Dae's hand stroked Ben's cock with increasingly erratic movements, and Ben's breath stuttered in pauses to the melody they played.

"Oh," Ben groaned as his balls constricted and his body flushed with heat. "I can't hold on anymore… God, Dae." His release spilled over them both, over Dae's hand and onto the sheets. He gasped at the overwhelming sensation his orgasm caused as Dae panted behind him.

"You look so debauched when you come. So beautiful." His thrusts were accompanied by a moan and a flash of wet heat exploding between Ben's cheeks, coating his backside in Dae's come. "Sweet mother of pearl, that was something else."

Ben missed Dae's warmth when his partner collapsed back onto the bed, chest heaving. He turned onto his back to face Dae, whose face was flushed and gleamed with perspiration.

"*You're* something else," Ben said drowsily. "I thought my dick was going to take off." He trailed fingers in the stickiness on Dae's lower stomach then teasingly licked them clean. Dae's pupils dilated as he watched. Ben loved the sense of power this little action gave him.

"I'm glad you enjoyed it." Dae shifted onto his side to stare into Ben's eyes. "I'm making it my mission to find creative ways to make you scream my name as you do."

"I don't scream your name," Ben pointed out in amusement. *At least, I didn't think I do.*

Dae chuckled. "I'm not going to argue with you. I can assure you, when we come to do the Beloved Badger, or Breaking Crow, you'll do more than scream my name. You'll sob in sheer ecstasy and beg me to do it again."

"Beloved Badger," Ben mouthed. "What the hell is that?" He couldn't deny the frisson of anticipation that threaded through his body like a red-hot wire.

Dae mimed zipping his lips, an evil glint in his eye. "Nope. You wait and see."

Ben huffed then sighed in contentment when Dae snuggled in under his arms and laid a hand on his stomach. Ben chuckled.

"We can't stay here all night. It's not the most comfortable bed and the cleaners will be here early in the morning. Come on, we need to clean up and get going."

Dae raised his head and huffed. "I was getting comfortable. Do we have to go now?"

"Yep. Come on, gorgeous. Let's gather our stuff and get out of here."

Ben stood and pulled Dae to his feet. They did some quick clean-up then Ben ushered Dae out of the offices and into the zoo grounds. The walk back to the car was pleasant. There was nothing Ben loved more than hearing the animals settling in for the night, or hearing the nocturnal ones chirping or growling. Or—was that the chitter-chatter of conversation? He frowned and listened carefully. It was coming from the aardvark enclosure they were walking past.

Perhaps someone had been left behind? Ben had often found kids hiding among the bushes along the path trying to sneak an after-hours preview of the animals. He nudged Dae, who was whistling softly under his breath.

"Give me a moment. I think someone's hiding over there. Damn kids."

Dae nodded sprightly and leaned against a lamppost along the path. "Go ahead. I'll wait here."

As Ben grew closer to the enclosure, the conversation grew louder. He still couldn't see anyone though, but whoever it was, was female with a soft, light voice.

"I said to him, he can't have it and he said, 'Why not, it's my bloody dinner, isn't it?'" There was a tut-tutting sound. "I said, look, love, you can afford to lose a bit of weight so let the little 'uns have the extra termites, all right? They need it more than you do."

There was a strange trilling sound from another part of the enclosure and another voice spoke. This one was coarser and deeper. "My George is the same. He's not only a lazy bugger, but he's also a greedy one too. We ladies have our cross to bear with our men, don't we?"

There was a snuffling sound and Ben leaned over the enclosure to get a better view. The area was dark, dimly lit only by a spotlight that remained on at night. Aardvarks were nocturnal and came out to forage. The only thing Ben saw were two aardvarks half in, half out of the light. Nothing was hiding there, or in the bushes around the enclosure.

How bizarre, he thought. Who the hell was speaking then?

One of the aardvarks looked up and stared at him. Ben squinted around to see better in case he'd missed anything.

"Well, would you look at that," the lighter voice said. "We have a late-night visitor. He's standing up there watching us. Bloody peeping Tom, I'd say. Hey, you up there. Mind your own business, will ya?"

Ben blinked once, then twice. The other aardvark looked over at him and Ben's skin prickled. What the fuck? Was the animal watching him?

"I see him there, Daisy. He looks harmless enough, like. Ignore him, he'll go away when he gets bored. They all do."

Both animals regarded him and Ben hitched a breath. He was close to hyperventilating and was sure he was losing his mind. Were the aardvarks speaking, and talking about *him*?

"Come on, Madge. Let's go inside," he heard next as both animals turned and ambled towards the burrow.

Ben knew he'd be looking at a stay in a nice white room if anyone found out about what he did next, but he had to know. "Are you talking about me?" he managed to get out finally.

The aardvarks turned around. "Do you see anyone else around here?" the deep-voiced one said grumpily. "We may be old, but we aren't crazy."

"Oh God," Ben said faintly. "They *are* talking. The aardvarks are talking." He turned and stumbled back down the path towards Dae. "Dae, the animals are freaking me out. They're talking about me. That's impossible, isn't it?"

Dae was still lounging against the lamppost and smirked. "You're asking a Fae turned Djinn if animals can talk. Don't you know nothing is impossible? Magic, remember?"

"You used magic on me?" Ben shrieked. "Why would you freak me out like that?"

Dae laughed loudly, the pealing sound echoing around the empty zoo. "I thought you deserved a reward for that fabulous sex session earlier, so I cast a little spell to allow you to hear the animals talk. You know, like that film we watched the other night only this time," he paused dramatically, "it's Doctor Daelittle." He giggled at his joke as Ben stared at him blankly.

"I thought I was insane, damn it. Next time tell me you're going to do your witchy thing and give a man a little warning."

"Where's the fun in that?" Dae countered as he flounced down the path towards the exit. "A man's job is to keep an air of mystery about him. And honey, do I have a lot of mystery inside me."

Ben followed his lover's slim figure, muttering beneath his breath. "Damned crazy person. He doesn't care if I end up in the funny farm or wearing stripes when I go to jail."

"I heard that," a voice boomed out of the zebra enclosure. "What's wrong with stripes?"

Ben didn't stick around to have another conversation.

He'd had enough for one night.

Chapter 14

Dae woke from a particularly fretful sleep and lay unmoving for a while, wondering what had woken him. The night was still, other than the sound of an owl hooting close by. April ushered in warmer weather—apparently unseasonably so, Ben had told him with glee. While a temperature of fifteen degrees Celsius wasn't anything to write home about in Dae's opinion, it was better than the cooler climes of a wet, damp March. Ben had insisted on leaving the window open, to let in the fresh air. Dae listened drowsily to the birds outside, willing himself back to sleep. Ben snored softly beside him, his hair framing his face. A tendril seemed to be tickling his nose, which twitched. Dae smiled and tenderly moved the offending hair away.

The clock on the bedside table read one a.m. Unable to get back to sleep, Dae got out of bed, careful not to wake Ben. *Time to make some herbal tea.*

He slipped his silky robe around his shoulders and as he passed the window, he caught the faint glow of something in the garden. Curious, he looked outside. What he saw sent tingles down his spine and he contemplated going back to bed and forgetting he'd ever seen it. After a minute, he sighed, popped his feet into warm slippers, and went downstairs. He opened the front door and stepped into the darkness, treading across the dew-speckled grass to meet his guest.

A woman sat on the garden bench under the willow tree, her pale blue aura a familiar sight. She whispered to something and raised her slim hands to the tree as if blessing it. For all Dae knew, she was. The woman was an enchanting sight as always. Dressed in deep sapphire blue robes, teamed with gold braiding, her white hair swept up behind an elegant neck in a chignon, she was the epitome of quiet, ageless beauty.

The greeting mantra left his lips instinctively, old habits and manners revealing themselves.

"Lady Mage Elicia. Welcome to this world. May your presence here bring solace to all that you touch, and your voice comfort those in pain. May you be protected by all that is earth, water, sky, and flame."

Dae stood, waiting to be invited to sit. The Lady Mage raised her face to him, a face creased with soft wrinkles and crow's feet, and smiled a gentle, loving gesture that took Dae's breath away and left him with a lump in his throat. *It's been so long since I was near anyone from home.*

"Daeliel Jadu Alario of Quimaria, of the race of Elliel, please, sit down. Your company would be most appreciated."

Dae sat down on the far end of the bench, not wanting to be presumptuous. The Lady Mage laughed and patted the place next to her. "Come, child, sit closer. Have things got that bad you must distance yourself from me?"

Dae shuffled closer and the scent of home invaded his nostrils. Lavender, the spicy scent of cinnamon, and fresh green grass. His eyes prickled with tears and he blinked them back. "Thank you, My Lady. It's been so long since we last met. I wasn't sure what the current court protocols were."

"Oh, child." The Lady's eyes grew sympathetic. "There is no protocol on earth that can stop me looking after people I care about." She reached out and took his hand. "Before we begin what I'm here to say to you, I must tell you this. Your family are well and thriving. They miss you very much and asked me to send you their love."

Dae's throat ached. "Thank you, My Lady. That brings me great comfort."

She nodded. "Your sister Jannalor is with child. She married her sweetheart, and they are good together. Your mother fusses over her, most pleased she is having a grandchild. Your father—" She laughed softly. "He is as always, grumpy but loving, and trying to pretend the idea of becoming a grandfather does not mightily please him."

Dae swallowed, his heart full. His family sounded as if they had moved on without him, something he was both pleased and saddened by. *It seems life does go on after all.* "They sound happy. I'm pleased for them."

The Lady's face grew serious. "You know why I'm here."

Dae nodded. "I suspected. It's about the wishes, isn't it?"

She sighed sadly. "Yes. My brother, the Lord, and the Lady feel you have had enough time here on Earth and are anxious for you to return to the lamp as soon as possible."

Dae gave a bitter laugh. "You mean they think I'm having too much fun and need to get back to my prison."

The Lady Mage shook her head. "On the contrary. They believe you being on Earth is punishment enough. They have no love for this realm, and to them it's probably more of a penance than being a Djinn in a lamp. However, as rulers, they have a responsibility to follow the rules of the Accord, which is absolute. That states the allotment of wishes is only open for twenty-one days from the Djinn first appearing."

Dae's chest constricted. "That's five days from now. You're telling me I have only five days left with Ben?" His heart beat faster at the news. "I've never heard of this rule. Is it a new one?"

The Lady laughed. "No, it's been the same for thousands of years. You didn't read the Accords Handbook, did you?"

Dae frowned. "It's three hundred pages. I skimmed what I needed to know." Like whether he was entitled to appeal his sentence. What kind of work he'd be doing while he was incarcerated, and whether he could have sexual partners while he was a Djinn or was it one of those ridiculous abstinence situations. He wouldn't have fared well with that last one.

The answers, in short, had been no, anything he wanted to do, and yes. After that, he'd not read much more.

The Lady's eyes gleamed with amusement. "Daeliel Alario, you are a precious gem in a river of pebbles and stones. I am pleased I interfered when your sentence was granted."

"About that. Why did you mitigate my sentence? Why was I special enough that you even tried?" Dae's brows furrowed. He shivered. Sitting outside in nothing but a flimsy robe was probably a bad idea. His balls had shrunk and his dick certainly wasn't enjoying the cold.

Lady Mage gave a secret smile. "I saw something in you, child. A future chance for happiness that needed nurturing." She scowled and Dae thought it was adorable. "That brother of mine and his wife lose their impartiality when it comes to their son. They were wrong to blame your relationship with Aether solely on you. I know that child. He was selfish and easily swayed, and his fear of disappointing his parents was his overriding worry when they found the two of you together."

"He threw me to the wolves," Dae murmured sadly. "I thought he loved me more."

The Lady scoffed. "By Beza's Beard, Aether loves no one more than himself. He didn't deserve a beautiful person like you as a life partner."

Dae's aching heart warmed at her words. "Thank you for your faith in me." He hesitated. "Can you not convince the Lord and Lady to give me more time?"

"I cannot. Not even I can waiver from the Rules of the Accord. I'm afraid five days is all there is left for you and your human."

"Five days," Dae said bleakly. "That isn't long, is it?"

Lady Mage inclined her head graciously. "It is not. In our time that is but a fleeting millisecond."

After that one millisecond, Dae would be placed back in the lamp to serve out the remainder of his five-year service. Where before that had seemed palatable, now it left a nasty taste in his mouth.

"You have feelings for this man, Ben Sinclair?" The Lady questioned. "He means more to you than a man whose wishes must be granted?"

Dae wasn't sure how to reply. "He is a good man. One worthy of the best life has to offer. It has only been a little more than two weeks, yet we have found a synergy and companionship I was missing, even with Aether. *His* loss no longer hurts as much as it did."

"Ah," The Lady said knowingly. "Have you fallen in love?" Her rosy lips curved in a smile.

"No," Dae spluttered. "Not quite. I mean, how can one do that in the short time we've known each other? Don't be ridiculous. We simply get on well. We are, erm, compatible in many ways. I wouldn't call that *love*."

He was blushing. He could feel it. He could also see Ben's soft lashes against his cheek when he slept, and the little thing he did with his nose when cuddling Tess.

The Lady nodded wisely. "I see. Well, it would bode well to encourage him to use his last wish before the time expires. After then, the wish is voided."

Dae's eyes widened. "Honestly, the wish *actually* expires? That sucks," he muttered. "Was that little snippet of information in the manual, too, in the small print?"

"It's on the first page, in rather large blue text, under the heading 'Very Important Things for a Djinn to know in Wish Granting,'" The Lady stated with a twinkle in her eye.

Dae huffed. "Still. Someone should have told me."

Lady Mage Elicia stood up, her dress rustling as she did so. "It has been lovely seeing you, Daeliel. I shall tell your family you are well. They will be thrilled to hear it, no doubt." Her warm hand caressed his cheek. "Speak to your young man. Convince him to make a wish and make it wisely. I'd suggest you both sit down and discuss your feelings for each other first. Who knows, out of such discussion, perhaps a solution may be found to both of your problems."

"What problems?" Dae asked waspishly. "He makes a wish, I go back to the lamp. That's about it." *Son of a Banshee, I don't want that to happen.*

The Lady cocked her head. "Is that how you see it? Silly boy. Perhaps I misjudge you. Think long and hard about what that last wish might be. I can offer you no more advice than that. Good-bye, Daeliel. May the energy and love of our beloved Nemesia be with you."

Dae stood. "And with you, My Lady. Thank you for the update on my family. It is appreciated."

Lady Mage Elicia shimmered and within moments she was gone.

Dae pulled his robe closer around his body, for all the good it did, and trudged back to the house.

His mind circled with questions.

The Lady sounded as if she expected Dae and Ben to come up with some magical solution to make life different for the two of them.

Dae sighed as he walked inside and closed the door. There *was* no magic solution. Dae was torn between wanting to remain here with Ben, and going back to serve the remainder of his sentence so he could eventually see his family—his niece or nephew for the first time.

He didn't think there was anything anyone could do to give him both.

***

"Why you in such a bad mood today, Mr Grumpy Pants? You've hardly said a word all day." Hemingway nudged Ben with his thigh as they sat together eating their sandwiches on the steps of the new work-in-progress monkey enclosure. At lunchtime today, the workers were enjoying their break in the sunshine on the grassy picnic area. Ben and Hemingway had the steps to themselves.

Ben shrugged. "I'm fine. Got a few things on my mind, I guess."

Hemingway looked at him shrewdly. "It's Dan, isn't it? Your cousin."

Ben didn't miss the slight emphasis on "cousin." He looked over at Hemmy. "What's that supposed to mean? Why would anything to do with Dan be giving me grief?"

Hemmy snorted loudly. "Ben, I've known you for a long time. Dan is your cousin like that pretty woman over there is your next bed partner." He gestured towards an attractive dark-haired woman walking past. "I wasn't born yesterday, you know."

Oh shit, Ben thought in a panic. Bloody Hemmy was too observant. "I'm sure I have no idea what you're talking about."

Hemmy grinned— a great big grin that showed his teeth and made Ben a little nervous. "Uh-huh. Don't fucking lie, mate. The two of you eye-fuck each other any chance you get. You two have chemistry. Hazel and I have noticed it. I don't know why you feel the need to pretend with us. We're your friends, and I promised Haze I wouldn't say anything, but…"

Ben heard the hurt in Hemmy's voice and sighed. The pretence was up and to be honest, it would be good to have someone to share his worries with. Even if he couldn't tell them the full story as they'd have him in a straitjacket before the day was out.

"Okay, so he's not my cousin. He's someone I care a lot about, and he's also the one causing my grey hair at the moment."

Hemmy punched his shoulder. "I knew it. Haze said I had to leave you until you wanted to talk about it, but this is better." He whooped with delight. "I *know* something she doesn't. Perhaps I should start an office poll about when you two are going to admit you're into each other, then pocket the winnings…"

His face creased in thought and Ben scowled at him. "Don't be an arse. I don't need anyone betting on my love life, thank you very much." He finished off his egg mayo sandwich and crumpled the plastic bag up to pop in his pocket. "Things are a little complicated right now."

Hemmy shoved the rest of his sandwich into his wide mouth and chewed. "That's what everyone says."

"Don't talk with your mouth full. It's disgusting," Ben said gruffly.

How the hell am I going to tell him anything without revealing the whole truth?

"So is his name Dan, then? Is he actually from Scotland? Because I have to tell you, mate, his accent keeps slipping." Hemmy burped and waved a hand at Ben. "Come on, spill the beans. I thought I was your bestie?"

"That remains to be seen," Ben muttered. "Why are you and Hazel so invested in my love life anyway? Haven't you got your own to deal with?" He couldn't resist. "Did you ever get a second date with that lass from Jamaica? The one who slapped you in the face and stormed out of the restaurant?" He snorted. "If you can call a McDonald's a restaurant."

Hemmy wiggled his bushy eyebrows. "Ooh, scorch. Yeah, that was a bit of a mess-up. She thought I was playing a joke on her, and we were going to Chez Donaldo, that fancy place in Fareham." He chuckled. "I still think I stand a chance with her, though."

Ben rolled his eyes. "Don't embarrass yourself any further, Hem. Leave that one be." He stood as the workers trailed back to the worksite. "Come on, let's get out of their way." He turned to look at the building behind him. "It's going up quickly, isn't it? It's going to look amazing when it's done."

Hemmy nodded as he stood, and they began their walk back to the central admin office to check what was next in their respective diaries. "I still can't believe someone anonymously donated a hundred thousand smackers to the zoo. I've never seen Hazel so happy. There's so much can be done with the money."

Ben hugged his secret to himself, along with a warm, tingly feeling in his chest he'd done something right. "It was a surprise all right. Almost magical."

"So, let's get back to you and Dan, then," Hemingway said as they walked down the winding paths to the main building. "Is his name really Dan?"

"No, his name is Dae. D-A-E. He isn't from Scotland, either. He's, um, from abroad."

"You and he are an item then? Is he planning on spending more time around here, maybe moving in?"

The ache in Ben's heart, one he'd forgotten about briefly from his banter with Hemmy, flared back up. "I'm not sure. That's half the problem."

"Tell me," Hemmy said softly. "You'll feel better talking about it to a buddy."

Ben sighed. "The past couple of days, he's been off. I mean, really quiet as if he doesn't want to be in the same room with me. I don't know what I've done, and he won't talk about it."

The tension at home was awkward and unmistakable. For two days, Dae had been uncommunicative, responding only in monosyllables and half-hearted enthusiasm to any of Ben's suggestions for dinner or going out. He also wasn't sleeping in Ben's bed anymore, a situation that hurt more than anything.

"I thought we had something special, but he's like another person. We've become strangers."

Hemmy hummed. "Sounds like something's troubling him. The few times I've met him, he's always been open and social."

"I've asked him what's wrong, he says 'nothing,' and gets this sad look in his eyes." Ben punched out at a leafy bush branch hanging in his way. "I don't know what to do."

They'd reached the building and mounted the stairs to enter.

"All you can do is keep showing him you care, and telling him whatever it is, he can share it." Hemingway squeezed Ben's shoulder in comfort. "He's head over heels for you, anyone can see it. Be patient and keep trying."

Someone called Hemingway's name and he moved towards them. "If anyone can get him to open up, you can, mate."

Ben watched him leave then turned to go into his office.

I'm scared he's going to leave me one day and I won't see him again. But he can't leave until I've made my last wish, can he? Ben had a terrible thought. *I wonder if there's an expiry period for wishes?*

He made a mental note to ask Dae about it when he got home. He'd make Dae his favourite cup of hot chocolate, with sprinkles, insist he sit down and then drag the truth out of him. He might be one stubborn Djinn, but Ben was stubborn too.

He wasn't going to leave Dae alone until he learned what was troubling him.

Chapter 15

Dae wasn't ready to hear the words he'd been dreading all day, ever since Ben came home.

"We need to talk." He'd known it was coming. Ben had a habit of loitering around looking as if he wanted to speak, then sighing heavily and finding something else to do. The dinner had been cooked, the dishes washed, and Ben had even taken the ironing board to iron a shirt for the next day. It was driving Dae crazy.

How do I tell him we have three days left before I have to go away?

Dae sat up on the couch, pulled his silky night-robe closer around his naked form, and sat back again. "What do we need to talk about? Have I done something wrong?"

Ben shook his head and sat down next to Dae. "No, not really. It's more what you aren't doing."

Dae raised one brow in question even though he knew damned well what Ben meant. "Oh? Tell me then." He picked up his chamomile tea. "I'm all ears."

Ben fidgeted nervously. "The last couple of days you've been…different. Distant, I mean, like you have something in your mind and won't share it."

Dae shrugged one shoulder. "I'm sorry. I didn't mean to be."

Ben reached out and took Dae's hand, rubbing it gently. "If something is bothering you, you can tell me. I thought we were partners."

Dae heart lurched. "Partners? How do you mean?"

Ben looked at him in confusion. "Well, you've been staying here with me for nearly three weeks now. We share a bed, we make love. I thought that meant we had some form of relationship."

Dae's heart cracked a little. "Ben, we do all those things, but you realise it isn't going to last, don't you?" He swallowed, trying to get rid of the lump in his throat. "You've known this is only temporary. We come from different worlds and I need to get back to mine."

Ben's eyes darkened. "I understand that. More than you know. It's been eating away at me because I'm not ready to end things." He sighed. "Why do you think I haven't made my second wish yet? As long as I hold back on it, you'll stay." His smile was beautifully sad. "Call it selfish, but I keep dreaming I'll find a way to keep you here."

Dae stood, unable to be too near to Ben. He wanted nothing more than to pull him close and hold him, and that wouldn't do. He needed to get the news out quickly, shock Ben like ripping a plaster off a wound. There was no other way to say it.

"You only have three days to make a wish. Then whether you make it or not, I have to go back into the lamp. Back to Calado'r."

Ben's face paled. "Three days? How the hell does that work? I thought it was up to the wisher to determine how long it takes. I'm not ready." He stood and paced around the room, his movements jerky, paired with his distress.

Dae swallowed. "No. Turns out I didn't read the manual properly. There are rules."

Ben turned to him, his expression angry. "How did you find this all out? Who reminded you of these 'rules'?"

"The Lady Mage Elicia came to see me the other night." Dae stared out the window towards the garden bench. "She sat over there," he pointed," and told me my time here on Earth had to end. The Lord and Lady had decreed it so, and I have to go back."

Ben's face twisted. "The Lady Mage Elicia. How come I didn't see her? Where was I?"

"You were sleeping," Dae muttered. "It was early in the morning and something woke me." He sat down on the couch again and pulled a cushion close to his chest. "She had news of my family and life back home. It was lovely to hear it, but then she told me the bad news."

Ben slumped down next to him, looking shattered. Dae's heart cracked a little more at the sight.

"So three days is all we have?" Ben's shoulders slumped. "I can't believe it."

They sat in silence. Tess came over and laid her head on Ben's lap, brown eyes soulful. Ben stroked her head absently. "Is there no way they'll grant an extension? I mean, I don't even know what to wish for."

Dae didn't answer, and shook his head in sorrow.

"Do you *want* to stay?" Ben asked abruptly. "I mean, is it something you'd consider? I know life here isn't exciting, and your life back home is more magical than this world, but you've become a part of *my* life. Is there some magic you can do to stay here?"

Dae sighed. "I've thought about it a lot the last week. I've come to love this world of yours, and then there's you. You make me feel life here could be fulfilling. But as a Djinn, I'm bound by the Rules of the Accord. They are the law where I'm from and cannot be broken."

He reached out and took Ben's cold hands in his. "It isn't on my list of things I want to do, but I have no choice. The Lord and Lady have decreed it. I'm being summonsed back to a further five-year sentence in the lamp, still without seeing my family or seeing you again."

They stared at each other in silence for a minute. Finally, Ben heaved a sigh and stood. He shuffled over to the window, his sweatpants and tee-shirt hanging loosely around him, and stared out into the dark.

"If you *could* stay here, would you want to?" His body tensed and Dae noticed his fingers clench at his side. "I don't want to make my final wish without knowing what your wishes are."

Dae puffed out his cheeks. "Ben, that simply isn't possible. It doesn't matter what I want."

Ben turned fiercely. "It *does* matter," he snapped. "I can't believe in all this talk of magic and other worlds there isn't a solution where you don't have to go back into that damned lamp prison. You're a Djinn, Dae. A being filled with mystery and wonder. Surely there must be something you can do." He sat and took Dae's hands in his. "The question is, what do *you* want to happen?"

Dae drew in a deep breath, his heart filled with anguish. "Ben, I don't know what I want, all right? I want to stay here with you, in this world, wake up to you each morning, play charades with your zany friends, and watch your face come alive when you're talking about your precious penguins. I want to see my family again, tell my parents I love them, and see my little sister grow up. What I *don't* want is to be the Djinn in the lamp with a life full of pleasure and excesses, but no one to love, no family, and subject to the whims of whoever next rubs the damn lamp. If there's a magic wish that helps me do all of that, then please, make it."

***

Ben couldn't help himself, and gathered his man in his arms and stroked his back with calm, soothing movements. "Baby, it's okay. I can't say I understand, because, hey, what the hell do I know about being cooped up in a lamp with no one to comfort me. I promise you, we'll figure this out."

He hugged Dae close, willing his warmth into his lover's body and wishing with all his heart he had the answers. Ben had a glimmer of an idea but he wasn't sure how Dae would feel about it. It would mean an incredible sacrifice, and Ben wasn't sure he could ask that of the man.

Dae pulled away and regarded Ben with troubled eyes. "I have a feeling you have a second wish in mind and aren't sure how to tell me about it." He smiled tremulously. "How about you lay it on me?" He leaned in and planted a soft kiss on Ben's lips then drew back and cocked a brow. "Well? Come on. Tell me."

Ben's insides churned. "I'm not sure I should. It's a bit of a selfish wish and assumes a lot."

Dae shrugged. "I won't know until you tell me, will I?"

Ben nodded. "Okay then. Here goes. Bear in mind I don't know how it would work, or if you'd want it to work, even if it is at all possible, but—"

"Ben, for fuck's sake, please stop rabbiting on and get to the point." Dae waved a hand in frustration.

"What if my last wish was for you to become human?" Ben blurted. "So you could stay here on Earth?"

Dae's jaw dropped. "Become human? Are you out of your mind? That would never work as a wish, and it's never been done before." He laughed bitterly. "Even if it did, how could I see my family if I wasn't allowed home?"

"I have no clue how this all works," Ben admitted. "I also remember you saying you had the power to grant a third wish at your discretion? What if I made that extra wish to allow you to visit your old world occasionally and see your family again?" He knew he was clutching at straws, but surely, if it hadn't been done before, there could be no precedent and therefore, perhaps room for some creativity from the powers-that-be?

"That has to be the strangest wish ever," Dae said, a faint smile on his face. "I'm not saying I don't like the sound of it, though." There was a look of yearning on his face. "If I could have the best of both worlds, I might even say make the wishes."

He frowned. "But what if you made them and they didn't work? I could get catapulted back to Calado'r without any warning, and neither of us would benefit. Although…" His expression grew thoughtful. "I did read *some* of the blasted manual and I remember it saying that all wishes had to be granted as they were requested, unless it contravened one of the many rules on health, sickness, bringing people back from the dead, etc."

"Is there any way you could ask your friend the Lady Mage what could happen before I make the wishes?" Ben asked. "So we didn't mess anything up?"

Dae looked at Ben. "Baby, we have only three days left," he said softly. "Whatever happens, I'm back in the lamp then, whether you make a wish or not. Whether any wish you make *works* or not. We don't have a lot to lose, do we?"

Ben's throat ached. "So, if we waited 'til the last minute, then I make the wish, we'd be no worse off. What do you think?"

He waited with bated breath while Dae considered the idea. It was a huge decision and Dae had the most to lose.

"Are you sure about this?" Dae caressed Ben's cheek. "Would you be ready to have me here with you permanently? Do you think what we have together is enough for us to make such a momentous decision?"

Ben had no doubts. "I love having you here, and I can't bear the thought of you leaving. I'd like nothing more than to come home to you each night."

Dae's face softened. "I feel the same. It scares the fuck out of me." He leaned in and took Ben's lips in a rich, passionate kiss, slipping his tongue into Ben's mouth with a familiarity that promised many more to come. Ben pulled Dae on top of him, clasping his hands on Dae's hips, loving the feel of the firm, fragranced body against his.

"We can have plenty more of this," Ben nuzzled Dae's throat, thrilling at the murmur of pleasure his partner made, "and this." His hand rubbed against the bulge in Dae's groin, encouraging Dae to press harder against his hand.

"And this." Dae smiled against Ben's lips as he slid a hand underneath Ben's shirt and tweaked his nipple. Ben groaned and thrust his hips against Dae's. Their cocks rubbed together and as their mouths explored each other's with hunger, Ben thought he'd rather be nowhere else.

"This isn't all we have," Ben murmured as he clutched Dae closer and their movements became erratic as they rutted against each other. "We have more than great sex in common. You know that, right?"

I think I'm falling in love with you if I'm not already there.

Dae pulled away and regarding him with glittering, heavy-lidded eyes filled with understanding. "I know," he said softly, nipping at Ben's bottom lip. "It's why I want to stay with you. You make me feel—cherished."

Dae's long hair fell about his face, tickling Ben's skin with its scented warmth. His hips rocked against Ben's in a cadence of slow, even movements, which caused Ben to lose his breath and gasp.

"That feels so good, baby. I'm almost there, don't stop, keep going. God, you drive me wild. You're so damned beautiful…" Ben's words tapered off as his cock released his desire into his sweatpants, leaving him shuddering with pleasure and biting down on his lip with the sensations in his belly and groin.

Dae grinned down at him wickedly. "I never tire of seeing you come," he whispered, his lips swollen, his pupils dilated and as dark as sin. "You look so sexy and debauched, and all I want to do is lick every bead of sweat and come off your body."

He sat up, all lithe beauty and shadowed limbs, the robe shifting on his body, revealing his hardened, flushed cock. "I want to feel you against me when I come." He pulled Ben's pants down his body, growling in pleasure at the sight of Ben's semi-hard cock.

"God, look at you. So bloody sexy, that gorgeous cock of yours. Sorry, this may feel a little sensitive but I need to feel your skin against my dick."

Dae hissed, eyes half-closed in an expression of bliss as he thrust harder against Ben's still-throbbing dick. "Fuck, baby, you do things to me no one ever has." Dae cried out as he spent himself against Ben, the flood of warmth against Ben's groin a welcome sensation.

Dae collapsed on top of him, a blend of warm flesh and muscled steel. Ben's hands slid down Dae's damp skin, bunching in the silk clinging to his lover's body.

"You magnificent bastard, you." Dae panted as he moved away and rolled over on the couch to lay tucked beside Ben's body. "What is it about us that sex always seems to be incendiary?"

Ben chuckled tiredly. "The force is strong between us, it is." He trailed fingers across Dae's stomach, absently gathering up the mess on his stomach and sucking it off his fingers. The look of lust in Dae's eyes promised more debauchery later.

"The force," Dae asked breathily. "Is that some obscure earth saying?"

Ben laughed. "Yoda. *Star Wars*." He rolled his eyes at Dae's confusion. "Never mind. It's one series we haven't got into yet." He drew a breath. "If you stay here, I promise I'll watch the whole thing with you. You'll love it."

Both of them smiled at each other, sensing the unspoken question beneath Ben's flippant answer.

Will they have enough time ahead of them to make the wish a reality?

Only time itself would answer that question.

Chapter 16

Dae shimmied his hips to the sound of "Rock DJ" and laughed when Hemmy attempted to do the same. The other man was bulkier and his attempts at sultry hip wriggling were adorable.

From the bar table, Ben watched them dance with a grin. He raised his beer towards Dae when he saw him looking. Dae focused on the music, trying to ignore the ache in his chest that told him tonight could be his last time on this earth for a long time. This could be the last time he saw Ben or any of his friends and enjoyed a beer while dancing in an incredibly packed establishment where a DJ wore an undertaker coat and a top hat. The quirks and vagaries of the human race never failed to tickle and entertain Dae.

"What's up, sugarplum?" Hemmy did a particularly violent hip bump towards young women on his left side, who laughed and bumped him back. "You haven't been yourself tonight." He glanced over at the table where Ben sat. "Come to think of it, neither has he. You two had a fight or something?" His dark eyes shone with interest.

Dae shook his head as he danced around his friend—*yes, Hemmy is my friend too*—and ignored the blatant lip licking and come-to-bed eyes from the well-built man dancing next to them. "No fight. I guess we're both a bit stressed right now. Lots going on, you know?"

Hemmy guffawed and performed an acceptable shimmy as he swayed towards the giggling group of girls dancing around him. "What the heck have you two lovebirds got to be stressed about? Ben's been a different person these last few weeks. You've been good for him, my friend."

Dae didn't answer. His skin warmed from Hemmy's description of him and Ben as lovebirds. It was lovely to know it wasn't one-sided and people noticed. As for stress, Dae snorted as he once again pushed the overeager guy in his personal space away, with a fierce scowl. Hemmy didn't know the half of it.

How about Ben having to make his wish, me being put back in a magic lamp, never to see him again, and having to live out the next five years on my own?

He mouthed at Hemmy, "I'm going back to Ben," and left the other man enjoying being the centre of attention amid the adoring female circle of dancers.

Ben smiled at him when he sat next to him. He pushed a drink towards him. "I thought you'd be thirsty so I got you one of those white wines you like so much." He reached up and pushed Dae's damp hair away from his forehead. "Wow, you had some killer moves out there. I was about to come out and deck that guy trying to crowd you." His tone was light but his eyes were stormy. "He seemed like a first-rate dick."

Dae waved a hand. "Pah. I've handled worse. But thank you for offering to come to my rescue. My white knight."

They smiled at each other, but Dae saw on Ben's face what was no doubt reflected on his own. A mix of sadness, apprehension, and longing.

Ben looked at his watch. "Not that I'm in a hurry to see you leave, but it's ten forty-five p.m. I know you said you had 'til midnight. I'd like to get home and prepare myself for whatever's coming. Fancy leaving?"

Dae nodded, a lump in his throat. "Yes, why don't you call a taxi? I'll go hug Hemmy and say cheerio." He took a sip of his wine and glanced at Ben. "Have you thought about what you're going to tell him when I'm maybe not around anymore?"

Ben shrugged. "The twisted truth, I guess. You had to go home to Scotland for some family emergency. I suppose I'll have to play down your absence." He offered Dae a twisted smile. "Let's stay positive, though. My wish will work."

Dae wasn't so sure, but he nodded brightly. "Okay." He stood. "See you in a bit."

It took a minute, but soon he was on the dance floor, telling Hemmy he was on his way home with Ben. Hemmy's grin was knowing—no doubt he thought the *lovebirds* were in the mood for some hanky-panky—but when Dae hugged him fiercely, almost choking back tears, he looked rather confused.

Dae strode back to Ben, who was now standing at the entrance. Together they exited the club into the chilled night air. Dae reached out and took Ben's hand. They stood silently as they waited for the taxi.

After all, Dae thought gloomily as they finally got in the taxi and headed for home, what was there to say?

***

Ben stared down into his mug of hot chocolate, watching the frothy swirls on the top. He and Dae had come home, made something warm to drink, and then Dae had left to do whatever he needed to do to ensure his last-minute belongings were safe somewhere in what he called "the ether." It was a sobering thought that this might be the last time Ben saw his lover's crazily decorated bedroom, or the strings of brilliant, jewelled lights strung around the room, and the deep purple drapes keeping the outside from intruding when they were both cosily ensconced in bed, making a haven for the two of them.

It might be the last time I ever see him.

Ben couldn't deny the pain pervading his whole body, and the prickling sensation at the back of his throat. *It has to work,* he thought determinedly. *It's my fucking wish and they have to grant it. That's the rules.*

When Dae came downstairs, his eyes looking a little red-rimmed, but with a forced sunny smile on his face, Ben's chest ached. He dredged up a grin and patted the seat next to him on the couch.

"Sit down, and let's do this." *God, I could put this off forever but that's not going to help either of us right now.* "First I have to ask, are you completely sure you want to do this? If it works, I'm asking you to give up your Faeness and your family. Is this world truly worth it? Am I worth it? This is a huge sacrifice."

Dae gave a jagged sigh. "I promise you I've done nothing *but* think about this. My mind is made up. I want to stay here with you." He sat and took Ben's hands in his. "It's half an hour to midnight, so yes, we'd better do this." He swallowed. "Are you ready to make your wishes?"

Ben took a deep breath and held both of Dae's hands in his. "I'm ready. I have something else to say first."

He gulped down his emotion. "These last few weeks have been incredible. I know it hasn't been that long, but having you in my life has meant the world to me." He paused as Dae's eyes shone with unshed tears.

Hell, Ben's eyes felt gritty and sore and he blinked furiously. "No matter what happens, I want you to know you're a man I could fall in love with. Hell, I'm already a little bit there." He took another deep breath. "If the worst happens, and you go back into the lamp, then if you ever find yourself back on Earth, you need to make me a promise to look me up."

He tried to smile but it wasn't quite there. "Wherever you find yourself next, I want you to make the best of it all, as I will. We owe it to each other to keep going and lead happy lives. Even if I will miss you like crazy."

Dae nodded as a tear rolled down his cheek. Ben wiped it off tenderly. "I promise all of that," Dae whispered. "I'll miss you too, Ben Sinclair. These last few weeks have been special to me. You've made me welcome in your world, and I hope I get to stay here with you, even if it means giving up who I was. I'll always be yours, no matter where I am."

He leaned in and for the next few minutes, Ben was lost in the feel of Dae's lips on his, the taste of salty tears and the warmth of skin against skin. When they pulled apart, Ben could hardly speak. Dae squeezed his hands comfortingly.

"It'll be all right. Say it," he whispered. "Say the words."

Ben's throat was dry, dread welling inside like the steady seep of a broken tap. But Dae looked so fearless right now, his eyes trusting, an expression of calm on his face.

Ben closed his eyes, then opened them again. Time to speak the phrases he and Dae had practised so often. Dae had warned him sometimes things got lost in translation when making a wish and the more detailed, the better.

"Oh Djinn of the lamp, please grant me my second wish. My wish is that Daeliel Jadu Alario, Elliel of the Kingdom of Quimaria, Djinn of Calado'r and son of Sameria and Medeaus, brother to Jannalor, be granted human form and the ability to remain on Earth, here with me."

He stopped and waited for Dae to do his bit. The granting of a third wish was something of a mystical process involving a lot of muttered words.

Dae nodded and closed his eyes, his hands waving in the air in strange circling movements interspersed with an occasional sharp clap. When he spoke, the language was like nothing Ben had ever heard before. It was captivating. Soft, hushed tones, the words an exotic chant of Middle Eastern dialects were mesmerising with their soft lilt.

Ben held onto Dae's shoulder tightly, dreading whether Dae would disappear into thin air suddenly. Who knew how this all worked? What he'd wished for was without precedent in the archives, and even Dae wasn't sure what would happen next.

To his relief, Dae seemed as solid as he'd been a minute ago, and when he'd finished his incantation, he nodded to Ben to say the next wish. They clasped hands, and Ben thought Dae was also as worried as he was that he'd suddenly vaporise and end up back in the lamp.

"Oh Djinn of the lamp, please grant me my third and final wish. I wish for Daeliel Jadu Alario, Elliel of the Kingdom of Quimaria, Djinn of Calado'r and son of Sameria and Medeaus, brother to Jannalor, to be granted access to his home world of Quimaria, that he may visit his family after he is human."

They both knew this was a tall order, but hey, they'd nothing to lose. That Dae had been willing to give up his family to stay with him had been humbling. Dae had said he had enough residual magic captured in a charm bottle to perhaps effect one last visit if the last wish weren't granted, but it was a gamble and there was no guarantee it would work.

Ben sensed a change in the air around them. They looked at each other as the room became scented with the faint perfume of jasmine and a haze began to rise from the ground, permeating the room with steamy clouds as it took over.

Ben grabbed onto Dae. *Oh God, is he disappearing?* He didn't seem as solid as a moment ago. Lethargy overtook Ben and he couldn't stop his eyelids from closing. He desperately tried to stay awake but something was taking hold of his senses and he could no longer resist the pull of sleep.

Perhaps if he had a quick nap, he'd wake up and everything would be fine. Perhaps this was the way it was all supposed to work.

That last thing he remembered was his hand dropping to his side as he lost his grip on Dae.

Then Ben tumbled to the floor.

**

Something wet and smelling vaguely fishy was licking Ben's face. He opened his eyes drowsily as a lolling tongue wet with drool lapped at his lips. It was gross, and Ben pushed the furry beast assailing him away with a shout of disgust.

"Ugh, Tess. Take that tongue of yours away, you beast. Only Dae's tongue has any right to be in my mouth." He shook his head groggily and sat up. As the fog in his head cleared, he realised what had happened before he passed out, and he shot to his feet, looking around in panic.

"Dae? Are you here?" The mist or whatever it had been was gone, and the only beings in the room were him and Tess, who sat at his feet, tail wagging.

Ben dashed out the door, into the hallway, calling Dae's name as he tore down the passage.

"Baby, are you here? Oh hell, please tell me you are."

It was a few torturous minutes later when Ben finally stopped, his heart breaking, and he faced the truth.

It hadn't worked.

Dae was gone.

Chapter 17

Dae awoke to the sound of tinkling bells, the scent of warm spices and sandalwood, and warmed air against his cheeks. He blinked sleepily then smiled, turning to snuggle up to Ben in the bed.

"Babe, have we overslept and we're in summer already? I think that's a good idea, hibernating through the cold winter—"

His eyes flicked wider open when he found nothing but space. He was alone on a bed of reeds covered with soft, fragrant moss. Covering him was a soft blanket made of fine wool. Apprehension tickled him with feather-light caresses and he sat up, now wide awake.

He knew this place. Knew it well. It had been the place he'd been sent to in despair when he'd learned he was about to be exiled from the Kingdom, sent to Calado'r away from everything he knew and loved.

The Lady Mage had comforted him back then and told him she was sorry she hadn't been able to help more. He'd cried until he was exhausted and she'd settled him on the reed mat with a promise to make his transition into the lamp as comfortable as she could. She'd been true to her promise even though his heart had been broken.

"Good, you're awake." The soft lilting tones of Lady Mage Elicia spun through his brain like strands of silk. "Welcome back, Daeliel Jadu Alario. My home is your home. May you find comfort and solace here."

She sat on a stool by the open window, through which sunlight streamed. Her dress of pale white lace and silver swirled around her as if a gentle breeze caressed her like a lover. Her pale blue eyes regarded him in sympathy, no doubt understanding his writhing thoughts. During their last conversation, she'd seemed to understand his feelings for Ben and the world he'd found himself in.

Dae sat up wildly, clutching the blanket to him like a life jacket. "My Lady. Thank you for your blessing." Manners were bred into young Quimarians, and even while Dae wanted to scream in anguish, his parents' teaching came to the fore.

Comfort and solace, however, wasn't what he wanted right now. Now he wanted answers. He wanted to be back with Ben, who was no doubt going into a full panic.

He cleared his throat and inclined his head graciously. "May I ask what my…erm…situation is?"

Please let Ben's wishes have worked. Sweet silver sands and by the beard of Beza, please let me be able to go home.

The Lady Mage's eyes gleamed both with amusement and compassion. "My child, did you think your Ben's wishes would be an easy task to grant? There is much to be discussed before they are fulfilled. Such wishes have never been made before and the Lord and Lady are in quite the turmoil about it."

Dae threw the blanket aside and stood up angrily. "I know one thing about the Accords, even though I may not have read it all, and that is all wishes *must* be granted. That is absolute. Would you renege on a sacred deal and the wishes of the Elders and Nemesia herself?" He stamped his foot and glared at her.

The Lady Mage laughed softly. "You are unique, Daliel. You fear no one and have no filter in that pretty mouth of yours. I am indeed heartened to see the passion you have for your life on earth." Her mouth thinned. "However, do I need to remind you that I am not to be challenged on the Accords or the will of Nemesia herself?"

Dae swallowed. He *had* rather had a meltdown and challenged someone who could turn him into an earthworm if she so fancied. Perhaps he should apologise. He opened his mouth to, and she held up a slender hand at him imperiously, indicating he should stay quiet.

"I am her mouthpiece here in Quimaria and respect is something I have earned. Don't you think so?" Her blue eyes sparkled with what Dae thought was anger. His heart sunk. He'd pissed off a powerful sorcerer and his only hope of getting back to Ben. Bane of Beza's Blight, why couldn't he have held his damned tongue?

He noticed the Lady's shoulders shaking. Ye Gods, had he made her that irritated she was about to summon up a tornado to cast him out into the Mire of Marlgamau, where people wore rags and lived in mud huts? The only mud Dae wanted to see was in his face mask.

"My Lady, my effusive apologies, I—"

She raised her head and Dae was dumbstruck—he was proud to admit that happened *never*—by the sight of her face creased in wrinkled laughter, tears streaming down her face.

"My boy, you are the most precious person ever. Did you think I was upset by your challenge? Your face, oh by Beza's Beard, it was a sight to see."

Dae's heartbeat slowed, but he couldn't deny feeling rather peevish. Honestly, this was all nothing but a joke?

"My Lady," he bit out darkly. "I am *so* glad I amused you. I was ready to prostrate myself on the floor to gain back your good graces. I'm so pleased now that isn't a thing because as clean as the floor is, I'm not convinced my beautiful form on your floor would do any favours to my clothing." He sniffed regally.

His snootiness made the Lady Mage laugh even more. He waited, beginning to see the humour in the situation, and his lips curled up unwillingly.

"Oh Daliel," she finally gasped. "Never change. You are a treasure to us all. Does the man you desire find you to be as adorable?"

Dae preened. "Well, yes, he does." He took a deep breath. "It's why I'm anxious to get back to him as soon as possible."

Her face grew serious. "That is what I wish for you too. But these things must be carefully handled." She turned and poured them both a glass of lemon-scented water from a jug on the side table. She handed him his drink and regarded him shrewdly. "You are quite correct saying that the wishes *must* be granted. But as you know, there are trickeries around the wording of wishes. Think back. Did your beloved ever ask for you to be permanently bonded to him in the other world, or was there perhaps a loophole to be exploited by those who would wish to do so?"

Dae realised with a sinking heart that perhaps there had been a loophole despite all their careful planning. Ben hadn't ever said that he wanted the transition to be permanent that he could recall. It had simply been a heartfelt plea for Dae to become human and remain with him. Length hadn't been mentioned.

"I…I'm not sure. I don't believe the word permanent was used, no."

She nodded wisely. "Then leave it with me. I will need to visit the Lord and Lady and put the case to them to grant the wish in the spirit in which it was meant. As for the second wish," she hesitated, "that will be more difficult. I am guessing you know that?"

Dae nodded, his throat choking up. "Yes. I know it has to be granted, but there was no talk of permanency once again." He clenched his fists in frustration. "I should have been smarter and realised what we were *not* saying. We worked so hard to make sure that the words were clear. I can't believe I forgot something as important as that." Hot tears filled his eyes and he slumped down on the second stool. "Ben must be so worried about me. It must be hours, even days since he's seen me by now. He'll be thinking the worst."

The Lady Mage laid a soft hand on his arm. "You are in love and were caught up with emotion. It is easy to make a mistake when one is blinded by such." Her tone was sad and Dae wondered if something similar had ever happened to her. "I will ask you to remain here while I discuss this with the Lord and Lady, and my superiors. There is also the situation of finding another Djinn to replace you should all Ben's wishes come true. I have a few who would truly leap at the chance so I doubt that will be too difficult." She patted his hand. "I will try my best to get you everything you want for yourself in the other world, Daliel. Stay positive." She stood with a rustling of clothing and another gentle smile.

"The lilies have bloomed again since you were last here. They are as beautiful as ever. Go visit them. I have no doubt they would welcome your presence."

Dae nodded, wiping away the wet from his cheeks. "Thank you, My Lady. I'm sure they'll cheer me up while I wait."

She gave him one last compassionate smile then was gone in a shimmer of soft haze. Dae sat on the stool, staring out into the exotic garden beyond, unable to enjoy its full splendour. He was drained, and wasn't the most patient of people, so waiting for a decision that would greatly impact his future was excruciating.

He stood wearily and exited the cosy home of the Lady Mage. It was as he remembered, a stone cottage with the cutest sloping room and a small side turret, set in the mountains of Adathra, amid the

Lakes of Evershire. It was a magical, mystical place inhabited by fae who preferred to live in peace and solitude rather than the hustle and bustle of trading towns and cities. It was also many moons away from his family.

The lilies were indeed as gorgeous as she'd promised. Fields of rich, creamy petals among a verdant landscape, their yellow inners releasing minute specks of pollen into the atmosphere. They seemed to whisper to him as he sat cross-legged on the grass under a shady tree and tried not to wonder what Ben was doing.

"I'm trying to come back to you," he whispered into the breeze. "Please stay hopeful. It's not over yet, I promise."

He desperately hoped what he was telling himself was the truth.

***

Ben put down his pen with a deep sigh and leaned back in his chair in his office at work. His back ached from sitting too long doing his damn monthly reports and looking at spreadsheets until his view became cross-eyed. It was almost six on a Monday night and he wasn't in the mood to go home. It wasn't the same since Dae had gone. It'd been over a week ago now.

"You have a dog to look after," he muttered to himself. "Get up and stop feeling so damn sorry for yourself." He was probably being harsher on himself that the situation warranted, but honestly, his life had grown dimmer. His days dragged on since the sassy light of his life had disappeared.

Ben closed up the office and headed home. He was riding his bicycle, enjoying the warmer climes and the later hour of the setting sun. As he cycled along the village lanes, all he could think of was Dae.

Neither of Ben's wishes had come true yet. The only thing Ben clung to when he went to bed alone at night was that Dae had been insistent the wishes *had* to be granted. It wasn't a case of them being ignored or cancelled once they'd been made. Ben held that fact close to his chest in the faint hope one day he'd get home and find Dae waiting for him.

Even if the powers that be granted his wishes with conditions, Ben was prepared to fight them, no holds barred. Of course, initiating a complaint with powerful magical beings wasn't going to be easy. He wasn't even sure how he'd do it. His ace in the hole was he still had the lamp and by God, he'd get Hemmy involved to rub the damn thing so they could make contact again with whoever made the decisions. Even if Hemmy had to wish Ben into the accursed thing.

That would certainly be an awkward conversation with his friend. As planned, Dae's absence had been explained to Ben's friends and colleagues as him having to leave suddenly for Scotland to deal with some family emergency. Ben hoped fervently Dae would return soon so his hare-brained scheme didn't become a reality. He could only imagine what Hemmy would say.

He shuddered at the thought.

When he walked into the house, only Tess was there to greet him, rousing herself from her dog basket to lick his hand and allow him a cuddle.

"At least *you're* here, old girl," Ben murmured affectionately as he prepared her food. He'd gotten into the habit of leaving kibble in her bowl to snack on while he was out of the house and giving her a tasty meal of canned lamb and vegetables when he got home, followed by a leisurely walk up the lane.

Later, Tess fed and walked, Ben was ready to put his feet up and lose himself in some mindless television. He found something on Netflix he fancied watching and escaped into the world of Eleven and her friends again in *Stranger Things.*

It was close to eleven p.m. when he made it to bed with his sleepy furry bed partner. He got comfortable, then placed a kiss on his fingers, then transferred it to Dae's pillow.

"Night, babe," he murmured before he snuggled in. "Hope everything's working out wherever you are. Sweet dreams."

***

Dae was antsy as hell after the rest of the day passed and the Lady Mage still wasn't home. The lilies were no longer doing it for him, so he'd taken a long walk, found a family of beavers building a dam in the river, a brightly coloured mushroom display, which he avoided like the plague, because even if they were pretty, yuck, mushrooms, and then skipped stones across the lake until he got bored. That had taken care of an hour. After that, he'd gone back to the house, found something to eat and hoped he hadn't been too forward, but he didn't think the Lady Mage want him to starve. He'd lain down on the reed mat to take a small nap. The small nap had turned into a few hours, and now he was awake, still groggy, and sitting outside in the sun, wondering what he could do next.

He'd been cloud watching, assigning shapes to them all: an erect penis and balls, a rather scruffy goat, and something that looked like a frog riding a bicycle. When he heard a soft swoosh behind him, he turned to see the Lady Mage standing at the entrance to her home. Her forehead was furrowed, her lips pressed together, and she looked thoughtful, which Dae took to be a good sign.

Dae's pulse beat faster as he stood and moved toward her. "Lady Mage, you're back." He didn't want to rush her about how she'd fared, so instead, he spurted out the first nonsense that came into his head. "Do you know clouds aren't weightless?" He'd learned a lot of facts about a lot of things watching *Blue Planet* with Ben, who loved any type of animal or nature programme. "An average cumulus cloud can weigh as much as a million pounds. Cirrus clouds are made of ice, not water." He pointed up at the sky. "They're quite fascinating things."

She regarded him in amusement. "Is that so? I agree. That's quite interesting." She entered the house and Dae followed her, his curiosity welling like floodwaters.

"So, how did it go?" he blurted out. "With the Lord and Lady?"

The Lady Mage flapped a hand. "A little give, a little take, like all worthwhile negotiations." She turned to face Dae, who was at the hand-wringing phase of this situation. He sat down on a stool and wrapped his arms around his knees so he wouldn't make a fool of himself.

"Uhm, what was given and what was taken?" he asked hesitantly. "Anything I should be worried about, or Ben?"

The Lady Mage shook her head. "Nothing that would concern you. Purely a favour owed." She poured another glass of lemon water for them, then sat down on her stool with a teasing smile. "I suppose you wish to know the result of my conversation with the Lord and Lady?"

"Oh yes, please," Dae said fervently. His heart was in his mouth as he waited.

The Lady took a sip of her drink. "It was easier than expected," she stated.

Dae's spirits rose at those words.

"As I mentioned to you before, they see remaining on Earth as more of a punishment than being in Calado'r, where you have access to magic, wealth, and everything else that makes it the wonderful place it is." She gave an unladylike snort. "They also feel your desire to be human is a fate worse than death. They cannot imagine anyone willing to give up their magic and their Fae life for one of mundane human existence." She cocked her head and regarded Dae with narrowed eyes. "The final sweetener is of course that, as a human, you'll never be able to set eyes on Aether again or tempt him when you are released from the lamp." She hesitated. "He is to be married to young Lady Annabelle next week. They have been courting for a long time and the Lord and Lady are anxious for grandchildren."

"Oh," Dae said faintly. "How nice for them." Strangely enough, the news made his chest ache only a teensy bit, but not like it would do if he were told he wasn't able to go back to Ben. Then his heart would explode and the fragments would be scattered far and wide.

"My Lady, you still haven't given the news I want." Dae stood. "Am I to be allowed to go back to Ben as human?"

He held his breath.

Lady Mage Elicia's eyes crinkled with satisfaction. "Not only are you going back as a human, my dear, but I also persuaded them to leave you with a little bit of your magic so you can visit your family."

Dae's legs gave out beneath him and he slumped to the floor on his knees, the overwhelming relief he felt sending a jolt of sheer joy through his body. "Oh, by Beza's Beard," he breathed, "That is incredible news, My Lady. How can I ever thank you enough for all you've done for us?" Hot tears trickled down his cheeks, but they were tears of happiness. "I can't even begin to tell you how grateful I am."

The Lady Mage stood and enfolded him a hug. "You deserve this," she murmured. "You were wrongly done by five years ago, and have been noble, and sacrificed much with grace. That I could do this for you makes me content." She released him and handed him a lace hanky to wipe his eyes. "However, there is a caveat to your visits to your family, I'm afraid. You can only come back once in a human year to see them. I was unable to get any further concession from the Lord and Lady."

Dae nodded. He'd take it. "I don't know what to say. I understand the condition and of course, I accept it."

She grinned slyly. "Be careful with that magic, little one. Try not to waste it on conjuring ghosts in haunted train rides, and making your poor lover think he is crazy when the animals engage him in conversation." She laughed, a sound like bells tinkling.

Dae's jaw dropped. *How the hell does she know about that?*

The Lady Mage winked at him and placed a finger on his chin, closing his mouth. "I know everything, sweet man. Now, close your eyes and I'll send you back to him. He must be missing you dreadfully."

Dae clasped her hand, his heart swelling with emotion. "My Lady—"

She silenced him with a finger on his lips. "Hush. You are welcome. I shall still be watching you, Daeliel Jadu Alario. You will always be in my heart. Close your eyes."

Dae did as he was bid.

***

"Hey, Ben, where do you want the rest of this meat?" Hemmy appeared round the corner of Ben's garden bearing a large tray of raw meat, set out with spice jars on the side.

Ben, busy at the gas grill with the chicken, motioned to the cloth-covered table to his right. "Pop it down there, will you? This is almost done. Then I'll put it in the oven to keep warm." He wiped his hands on his BBQ apron, one Dae had bought him with a dishy naked man on it, hands strategically placed over the groin.

God, I wish Dae was here. He'd love this. A warm spring day with all our friends around. Where are you, baby? I miss you.

Truth was, he'd begun to doubt Dae would ever come back. It had now been nine days since he'd disappeared, and every morning Ben woke alone, hope dwindled.

Hemmy set the tray down and sauntered over to Ben, two beers in his hands. He handed one over. "Here you go, I noticed you were dry." He watched as Ben expertly turned the chicken to crisp the skin. "You heard from Dan?"

Ben shook his head. "Yeah, he's good. Still sorting things out up there. Hopefully, he'll be home soon." He took the chicken off the grill and slid it onto a clean plate. "That can go inside. I'll put the rest of the meat on to cook."

"Hey, Ben, can you be the voice of reason please?" Hazel and her newest partner appeared at Ben's side. "Raj is telling me to use creme fraiche in my beef stroganoff and I still think there's nothing better than proper cream. I know you've made this dish before, what do you think?"

Ben shrugged. "I prefer to use sour cream because it's not as calorific as creme fraiche. It's a personal thing, so you're both right unless you're watching your weight." He grinned. "Which you always seem to be doing, Haze. I don't know why. You're perfect as you are." He slid another piece of steak onto the grill and watched in pleasure as it sizzled and spat.

Hazel preened. "Aww, you say the sweetest things."

Raj chuckled and put his arm around her. "I tell you the same thing and you tell me I'm a liar? He says it and you call him sweet?"

Ben prodded Raj with his spatula. "Welcome to relationship wiles, my friend."

Someone tapped him on the shoulder. "Ben, have you seen Mal? He went off to get me another drink and I can't find him."

Ryan stood, swaying slightly on his feet. His dark hair was mussed, his lips pouty. Ben surmised Ryan and Mal had been holding an epic make-out session somewhere. Ryan's new boyfriend was slim, cute, and had green hair. Ryan was enamoured with him, and Mal with Ryan. They were adorable.

"He went into the garden hut to grab an extra deck chair." Ben waved over towards the hut at the bottom of the garden. "I haven't seen him come out yet, though. Maybe you were supposed to join him?" He winked at Ryan, who smiled sunnily.

"Oh, you think? Thanks, Ben." He tottered off to the hut, and Ben shook his head in amusement. No doubt Mal had an ulterior motive for disappearing.

Hemmy laughed. "That boy has had enough to drink, I'm thinking. Time to cut him off."

Ben looked around for his special steak spice. He couldn't see it anywhere and handed the metal spatula to Hemmy. "Here, take over for a minute. I need my super spice to season these steaks."

He scooted off to the kitchen, passing Hazel and Raj making out on the garden bench under the rose trellis. Ben felt a twinge of envy. He wanted to be doing that, kissing Dae until their lips were numb, and making love in the bed upstairs until both of them lost their minds.

Dae, you'd better be home soon, no matter what, because I can't do without you. Please come home. Please.

"Where are you," he muttered as he searched the cupboard. "I know I saw you here the other day. Where the hell are you?"

"Right behind you," came a soft reply.

Ben stood stock-still, heart thundering in his chest, hoping beyond all hope he wasn't dreaming that familiar voice.

"Aren't you going to turn around?" the voice asked in amusement. "I've been gone a while and all you can do is stand there?"

"Dae," Ben gasped and turned so fast he thought he might have injured his neck. "You're back."

Dae nodded. "I am. I'm not going away from you ever again." He looked a little tired, but he was still Dae. Dressed in soft yoga pants and a clear, lemon-hued chiffon top, he was a beloved sight, and Ben wanted to whoop for joy.

Instead, he hurled himself at his lover, wrapping him up tight, finding his mouth with the desperation of a fish out of water. Dae's hands encircled Ben's waist as they pulled together like magnets, and the warmth and passion of their kisses catapulted Ben to that place he felt most at home. In Dae's arms.

When they'd quieted their immediate need to kiss each other senseless, they pulled apart and Ben held Dae's face in trembling hands, not willing to let him go.

"You were gone so long, I thought it was over," he whispered against Dae's fragranced hair. "God, I missed you so much. I didn't think it was possible."

"It took some time to get things resolved, but the Lady Mage got the wishes granted, and a replacement Djinn settled in." Dae reached out a hand and gently stroked Ben's new trimmed beard. "I like this. Not too much. Very sexy."

"I've been a little lazy about shaving," Ben confessed. "God, I'm so relieved you're home. The guys are going to love seeing you again."

"The guys?" Dae frowned. "You have visitors. Who are they?" His beautiful lilac eyes narrowed. "Have you replaced me so soon?"

Ben shook his head. "No, doofus. I'm having a barbeque, and Hemmy, Hazel, and Ryan are here with their significant others. Well, Hemmy doesn't have one because honestly, he can't choose from them all. One day that man is going to find an irate husband waiting for him around a dark corner."

He'd only had one beer, but he was giddy with happiness. He drew Dae over to the lounge and pushed him down onto the couch. "Tell me about my wishes. What happened?" He sat down next to his man and waited.

Dae smiled softly. "All you need to know is that as of midnight tonight, I'll be human. I'll be able to stay here with you and we'll grow old together. If that's what you want."

"Hell yes, that's what I want." Ben captured Dae's lips in another kiss. "I've dreamt about you coming home. You've sacrificed so much to be here with me. I can't even tell you how much I love you for that."

Dae's eyes shimmered in shades of purple. Ben was entranced by the emotion shown in them. "You love me?"

Ben cupped his face. "I love you. You're mine. My beautiful, incredible genie."

"Not anymore," Dae said wryly. "Although I do have a little bit of magic left in me." He closed his eyes and lifted his fingers, and above their heads, a ring of fairy lights flickered, rotating in the air like a crown of fireflies.

Ben stared at it in awe, then back at Dae. "So you'll be able to visit your family?"

Dae nodded. "Yes. Once a year I can go back. It was the best she could do. They will be sad I've made this decision, but I'm happy with it. As long as I have you." He leaned in and kissed Ben on the cheek. "I love you too. This is my new home. Here, with you and Tess." He waved a hand at the backyard. "Those people out there. Our friends. I look forward to getting to know them much better over the years." His face shone. "It feels good to be able to say that."

"I can't believe you're back. Knowing we'll grow old together."

Dae leaned in close to Ben and whispered, "She let me keep the tattoo as well, so your fetish can still be served." He grinned. "The new Djinn got an elephant tat. She seemed pleased with it."

Ben stood up, dizzy with relief. "While I want you madly, and nothing would delight me more than taking you to bed right this minute, I have food on the grill and Hemmy isn't the best at turning the meat on time. I want to take you outside, show you off, and let everyone know you're home. Is that all right?"

Dae pursed his lips. "More than all right." He pouted. "I feel I should have dressed up a little more, but this outfit will have to do."

Ben chuckled. "There's my fashion-conscious man. Come on." He took Dae's hand and tugged him towards the garden. "I must warn you. I think Ryan and Mal, his new partner, are having sex in the garden hut, and Hazel and Raj were getting frisky when I passed them earlier. Hemmy's probably out there watching it all, and there could be a fire in the garden if he hasn't paid attention to the meat. Just saying."

Dae looked a little shell-shocked at having all that information in one fell swoop.

Ben flashed Dae a huge smile.

"Welcome back, baby. This is just the beginning."

TURN THE PAGE FOR A SNEAK PEEK AT
GIN ME OVER

GIN ME OVER

The day had started well enough, but as we all knew, unexpected events can soon lead to disaster. I stared in horror at the woman lying face down in a mud puddle, her stockinged legs splayed ungainly while she cursed like a biker chick. Her vocabulary was certainly…colourful. Not what I'd expect from a bank employee here to advise me on business affairs.

Beside me, my shop manager and friend, Valerie Vickers gawped in dismay, her gaze flicking from me to the large, preening peacock strutting around the garden. I supposed I'd better try and put some essence of discipline into the awkward situation.

"Bad bird," I admonished helplessly. "You should be so ashamed of yourself, King Lear. You've been a very, very bad peacock."

I'd offered to help the unfortunate mud-spattered woman, but she'd growled at me and told me to leave her the fuck alone. I'd backed off, of course. I was a gentleman, after all.

"God, I'm so sorry this happened to you, Ms Greer," Val said as she reached out a and to help the lady up. "The bird isn't usually that ferocious. I don't know what came over him to chase you like that." She glared at me again while she helped Polly Greer to her feet. I wasn't sure why *I* was in trouble. King Lear had never chased anyone before, and I couldn't account for his actions.

"That animal is dangerous. How can you have such a bird on your premises when you have customers?" Polly's high-pitched voice made King Lear give her the beady eye, and I moved swiftly to wedge myself between them in case he decided to charge her again.

"He's a peacock," I offered helpfully. "They can be quite territorial." I winced when Val pinched my upper arm.

"*Not* the time for a nature lesson, Birdy," Val said between clenched teeth. "Now get that damned bird out of the way while I help poor Ms Greer inside to clean up. I think she needs a cup of tea too. Come with me, dear."

I watched as the two women walked up the cobbled garden path to the main store. There *was* a positive side to this unfortunate event.

I didn't have to sit and listen any more to Ms Greer talk about downsizing and making employees redundant. She'd had a one-track mind and after revealing her master plan for the benefit of my business—without any benefits I could see, mind you—I wasn't altogether sad she might not come back.

"If I could fist bump you, dude, I would," I murmured to King Lear as I held out a piece of his favourite ginger cake to lure him back into the pasture far away from the store. I always carried a bit of something sweet in my pocket, either for King or to feed the birds I saw on my travels. "But I don't condone your behaviour, do you hear me? You can't go around scaring poor women into falling into mud puddles. It's just not done."

King Lear squawked loudly, and I winced at the sound. "I understand you thought you were doing me a favour, but don't do it again, okay? I'll probably be sued by the bank now," I muttered gloomily, "for causing stress and damage to one of their employees. God, I hope that doesn't happen. I don't need any excitement in my life."

When King Lear was far enough away from the main store and could be deemed no more danger to anyone, I threw him the rest of the ginger cake and ambled back up to the shop.

Time to make reparation for my wayward bird and see if anything I could do would keep future trouble away. Perhaps I could offer Ms Greer a nice bottle of our expensive Blueberry Explosion gin. That should calm anyone's nerves.

ABOUT THE AUTHOR

The 'Official' stuff

Susan writes steamy, sexy, and fun contemporary romance stories, some suspenseful, some gritty and dark, and she hopes, always entertaining. She's also Editor-in-Chief at Divine Magazine, an online LGBTQ e-zine, and a member of The Society of Authors, the Writers Guild of Great Britain, and the Authors Guild in the U.S.

Susan is also an award-winning screenplay writer, with scripts based on two of her own published works. *Sight Unseen* has garnered no less than five awards to date, and her TV pilot, *Reel Life*, based on her debut novel, *Cassandra by Starlight*, was also a winner at the Oaxaca Film Fest.

The 'Unofficial' stuff

Susan loves going to the theatre, live music concerts (especially if it's her man-crush Adam Lambert), walks in the countryside, a good G and T, lazing away afternoons reading a good book, and watching re-runs of *Silent Witness*.

Her chequered past includes stories like being mistaken for a prostitute in the city of Johannesburg, being chased by a rhino on a dusty Kenyan road, getting kicked out of a youth club for being a bad influence (she encouraged free thinking), and having an aunt who was engaged to Cliff Richard.

Connect with Susan:
website: authorsusanmacnicol.com
facebook: Author-Susan-Mac-Nicol
twitter: SusanMacNicol7
instagram: susiemax77
linkedin: susanmacnicol

www.BOROUGHSPUBLISHINGGROUP.com

If you enjoyed this book, please write a review. Our authors appreciate the feedback, and it helps future readers find books they love. We welcome your comments and invite you to send them to info@boroughspublishinggroup.com. Follow us on Facebook, Twitter and Instagram, and be sure to sign up for our newsletter for surprises and new releases from your favorite authors.

Are you an aspiring writer? Check out www.boroughspublishinggroup.com/submit and see if we can help you make your dreams come true.